Sébastien Japrisot was a prominent French author, screenwriter, film director, and the French translator of J. D. Salinger. He is best known for *A Very Long Engagement*, which won the Prix Interallié and was made into a film by *Amélie* director Jean-Pierre Jeunet. *One Deadly Summer* won the Prix des Deux Magots in 1978 and the film adaptation starring Isabelle Adjani won the César Award 1984. *Rider on the Rain* was also made into a film starring Charles Bronson. Born in Marseille in 1931, Japrisot died in 2003.

Linda Coverdale has a Ph.D. in French Studies and has translated over eighty books, including Japrisot's *A Very Long Engagement* and works by Marguerite Duras, Jean Echenoz, Emmanuel Carrère, Patrick Chamoiseau, Georges Simenon and Roland Barthes. A Commandeur de l'Ordre des Arts et des Lettres, she has won many awards, including the International IMPAC Dublin Literary Award and several Scott Moncrieff and French–American Foundation Translation Prizes. She lives in Brooklyn, New York.

Rider on the Rain

Also available from Gallic Books:

Rider on the Rain

SÉBASTIEN JAPRISOT

Translated from the French by Linda Coverdale

Gallic Books
London

A Gallic Book

First published in France as *Le Passager de la pluie* by
Éditions Denoël, 1992
Copyright © Éditions Denoël, 1992

English translation copyright © Linda Coverdale, 1999
First published in Great Britain in 1999 by the Harvill Press
This edition first published in 2021 by Gallic Books, 59 Ebury Street, London,
SW1W 0NZ

ISBN 9781913547134

Typeset in Adobe Garamond by Gallic Books
Printed in the UK by CPI (CR0 4YY)

Either the well was very deep, or she
fell very slowly, for she had plenty of
time as she went down to look about her,
and to wonder what was going to happen next.

Lewis Carroll
Alice's Adventures in Wonderland

Tuesday, 5 p.m.

1

A peal of thunder, a grey river spattering in a downpour, a horizon blurred by autumn. And then the wheels of a bus send up great glistening sprays of water, and the river becomes a road running the length of a desolate peninsula, somewhere between Toulon and Saint-Tropez.

From quite high up, well above the housetops, we watch the vehicle – which is grey, like the road – entering a deserted seaside resort: Le Cap-des-Pins. As we can see, it is not even a town, actually, but a single long street that follows the curves of a sandy beach battered by the chilly Mediterranean.

There is no one in the street. There does not seem to be anyone on the bus. There is only the rain, falling steadily and heavily, and the movement of massive waves breaking on the shore.

At the end of the street, a large crossroads: a supermarket, closed; some summer shops, also closed. One road heads inland through vineyards, while another, edged with streaming palm trees and shuttered houses, follows the coastline.

It is at this crossroads that the bus stops.

From the other side of the street, behind a window lashed by sheets of rain, a young woman watches the bus pull up.

She is blonde, pretty, wearing a white turtle-neck sweater. White suits her. She is twenty-five years old. She has a sensible haircut, a sensible face, a sensible life, and doubtless, in her heart, dreams as crazy as everybody else's, but she has never told them to anyone.

She is Mélancolie Mau, known as Mellie, and later on someone will call her 'Love Love'. Her expression, her bearing, even her temperament, are in perfect accord with her real first name.

At this moment, however, as she looks through the window, she presses a finger of her right hand against her lips, allowing us to notice the one thing about her that belies her serene and well-groomed appearance: nails bitten to the quick.

A woman's voice is suddenly heard behind her, loud and incredulous.

'Mellie? … Is that the bus from Marseille stopping here?'

'Yes, Mummy.'

'Certainly not. That bus never stops.'

She speaks with the assurance of someone who would never permit even obvious facts to change her mind. Mellie does not reply. Besides, the bus has halted for only a few seconds. It is already pulling away from the kerb.

The room where the young woman watches from the rain-streaked window is somewhat lower than the street, so that she sees the bus from the side and on a level with the wheels.

Only the driver is on board, but as the heavy vehicle moves away, it reveals a passenger she had not seen get off the bus, standing motionless in the rain.

He is quite tall, with a shaven head, and seems uncertain, like someone arriving there for the first time. He is wearing a grey raincoat and carrying a red travel bag – one of those canvas overnight bags given away by airlines.

The woman with Mellie calls out again.

'What are you looking at? Is there a passenger?'

'Yes, Mummy.'

'Did he come in on the bus?'

As the question is not worth answering, Mellie does not reply. It is her mother who answers her own question, peremptorily.

'Certainly not. No one ever comes here on that bus.'

Mellie gives a slight shrug, still watching the stranger across the street. Before turning away from the window, she replies amiably, 'Then he must have ridden in on the rain.'

Outside, the man hesitates, paying no attention to the raindrops running down his face. He looks at the sea. He even takes a few steps in the direction of the departed bus. And then, thinking better of it, he heads back towards the centre of the village.

He walks slowly along beneath the dripping pine trees, staring straight ahead of him, like someone who has no idea where he is going, and his red bag is the only spot of bright colour in the driving rain.

2

A white sports car going at breakneck speed skids suddenly and horribly out of control on a dark road. After turning over three times, the car comes to rest against a woman's hand blocking its way – a real hand, larger than the car.

This hand picks up what was only a toy on an electric track and sets it down on one side.

In the harsh glare of an overhead light, the mother of Mellie Mau lights a fresh cigarette from the fag-end of the one she is just finishing.

A woman still youthful and elegant, she has a nervous, affected manner. She is one of those people who, hating everything, hate themselves. Her name is Juliette.

She is sitting at an immense table on which is mounted a racetrack for miniature cars, with bridges, zig-zags, and steeply banked turns. Although it is not yet dark outside, the spotlights above this table have been turned on.

Mellie Mau is seated on the other side of the table and watches her mother stub out her cigarette in a full ashtray.

MELLIE: That's the third one in ten minutes.

JULIETTE: I smoke so that you'll have something to say to me.

She almost always speaks in a sharp, even disagreeable tone, but without raising her voice or taking any notice of other people's reactions.

She is busy checking her cars. She places the damaged ones inside a large cardboard box sitting open beside her.

MELLIE (*in a hurry to leave*): I have to go and pick up my dress.

JULIETTE: I've finished.

They are alone in a vast basement with an arched ceiling – a kind of funfair for summer visitors, the sort of place found everywhere along the coast: a bar with rows of bottles arrayed behind the counter, a few slot machines, two pinball games, and a jukebox. But it is the four bowling lanes of pale varnished wood, superbly maintained, that take up most of the room.

The amusement hall, which is called 'Chez Juliette', is closed until Easter. All the windows are tightly shuttered, except for the panes in the door opening onto the street.

Juliette tests one last car by lifting its back wheels off the track and accelerating to top speed. She places it among those in good working order.

JULIETTE: There are six that need to be repaired. What's wrong with that one?

She reaches across the racetrack for the red car Mellie Mau is holding. The young woman leans out beneath the spotlights to hand it to her.

MELLIE (*standing up*): It flips over.

JULIETTE: Certainly not. You never know how to do anything!

Without answering, Mellie picks up a white raincoat draped across the seat of a chair and puts it on.

Her mother walks barefoot across the bowling lanes and steps behind the bar. She pours herself a whisky. Neat, no ice.

Mellie watches her but says nothing. She closes the box of cars to take it with her.

JULIETTE: Well, say it – I drink too much!

MELLIE: Mummy, you drink too much.

JULIETTE: I drink to forget.

Looking grim, she takes a big gulp of her drink.

MELLIE (*wearily*): To forget what?

JULIETTE: That men are bastards.

In her white raincoat, rainhat, and matching boots, Mellie heads towards the door, carrying the large box under one arm.

JULIETTE: Those damaged cars, when will you take them in to be fixed?

MELLIE: Day after tomorrow.

JULIETTE: Why not tomorrow?

MELLIE: Tomorrow, I'm going to a wedding.

JULIETTE: You mean your husband doesn't want you to see me.

MELLIE: He doesn't want me to come here; that's not the same thing.

Opening the door, she stands for a second before the pelting rain. When she turns back to her mother, her face is already wet.

MELLIE: Besides, you're invited tomorrow, too. Why don't you just come?

JULIETTE (*without looking at her*): I went to mine, and that was enough, thank you.

A faint sigh, a nod, and Mellie leaves.

MELLIE: Bye, Mummy.

It is only after the door has closed that Juliette looks up and replies.

JULIETTE (*with unexpected tenderness*): Bye, darling.

She downs the rest of her drink in one swallow.

3

Dashing through the rain with her big cardboard box, Mellie Mau reaches a car parked in a lay-by on the other side of the street, facing the sea.

It is a midnight-blue Dodge Coronet station-wagon, luxurious, but muddied by the bad weather.

Mellie shoves the box into the boot and hurries to get behind the wheel.

A moment later, she is driving down the long street of Le Cap-des-Pins.

She drives slowly, and the size of the car, as it rolls smoothly and silently along, reinforces that impression. The only sound is the splashing of the rain.

Behind the to-and-fro of her windscreen wipers, Mellie passes through a deserted village. Only a *bar-tabac* is open.

It is in front of this bar that the man from the bus is standing with his red bag.

The lights inside the bar have already been turned on for the evening, and some customers are playing cards. But the stranger has not gone inside to take shelter. He is standing absolutely still on the pavement, in the rain.

As she drives by, Mellie Mau glances at him through the side window and their eyes meet. He has the eyes of a statue, silent and grave, as impassive as his rugged face.

She cannot help looking back at him in her rear-view mirror. She sees that abruptly, but without haste, he begins walking again, in the direction that she is going. He is still carrying the red bag.

She thinks no more about him.

Further on, where the road leaves the village, another window is lighted. The shop sign says, NICOLE BOUTIQUE. Mellie stops the Dodge, and, slamming the car door behind her, runs into the shop.

A few moments later, a curtain of heavy beige material is pulled aside, revealing the young woman getting undressed. Three mirrors reflect her image as she begins peeling the turtle-neck sweater off over her head.

She is in the changing cubicle of one of those shops where bathing suits, dresses, trousers, blouses, and whatever else can be sold to female tourists during the summer months, all pile up in a heap on five square metres of thick carpet within four walls of white pebbledash.

The hand drawing back the curtain on Mellie Mau belongs to Nicole, the proprietor and sole employee of the establishment, and Mellie's longtime best friend.

Nicole brings over a dress on a hanger. It is a white cocktail dress with a flared skirt, and it fastens from top to bottom with a row of crystal buttons.

Nicole is the same age as Mellie, or only slightly older, but her years of experience count for double.

She is a good-hearted girl who tries to be cheerful and is sometimes sad; she is attractive, intelligent, sensitive, and she would make some man – as is said of girls who have not yet had to prove it – very happy. In a word, she is single.

She hangs the white dress inside the cubicle, and talks to Mellie whilst helping her wriggle out of the turtle-neck.

NICOLE: They can go to the Moon all they want, and to Mars, and to Wherever, but they still won't find anybody up there. Anywhere. So what's the point?

MELLIE (*freed from her sweater*): Did you get the bread I wanted?

NICOLE: Yes, I got your bread. It's over there.

She moves away from her friend, who is taking off her skirt. As Mellie carefully folds up her clothes, she studies the white dress hanging in front of her.

MELLIE: You don't think this dress is a bit short?

NICOLE (*crisply*): No.

MELLIE (*taking off her boots*): Give me your shoes so I can check.

Nicole steps out of her high-heeled shoes and, with one bare foot, pushes them over to Mellie, who slips them on.

NICOLE: That husband of yours doesn't like short dresses?

MELLIE: Not on me he doesn't.

She undoes the buttons of the dress on the hanger, one by one, sometimes stopping to examine the seams.

NICOLE: When's he coming home?

MELLIE: Tony? Tonight.

NICOLE: He's supposed to bring me back a record, from London. You've no idea ... *Slin*-ky!

Reflected in three mirrors, Mellie gives a little laugh as she takes the dress off the hanger.

MELLIE: What's that like, a 'slinky' record?

Nicole claps her hands softly and hums a slow rock tune. She does a few sensual dance steps for her friend out in the open space of the boutique.

Doing this, she moves away from the cubicle. The beige curtain is only half closed.

Mellie Mau, undressed, suddenly notices in a mirror that there is no longer a screen between her and the shop window and that a man is standing on the pavement, motionless, watching her.

She whips around.

The incident would be a brief and unimportant one, were it not for the steadiness of the man's gaze. It is the stranger from the bus.

He does not turn away or walk off like a voyeur caught in the act. Standing there in his soaking raincoat, holding his red bag in his arms, he stares unblinkingly at Mellie Mau with eyes that devour her whole, yet not a flicker of expression crosses his face.

She is transfixed, as if mesmerized by his own fascination.

All she would have to do is pull the curtain closed. For one, two, three seconds, locked in a look that lasts forever, she is incapable of doing this. In fact, she discovers what is most paralyzing for someone like herself: the abnormal. This man is abnormal. She sees it in his eyes, she senses it, she knows it.

But there is something else. She is not naked, or simply half-undressed. She is wearing an outfit – stockings, suspender belt, pants, bra, and Nicole's damned high heels – that suddenly takes on, in spite of her having worn such things for years, a disturbing and almost culpable reality: it is because of this outfit that she, Mellie Mau, is fascinating to an abnormal man. And she sees that in his eyes as well.

Three seconds pass during which Nicole can still be heard humming, unaware of what is happening.

And then Mellie yanks the beige curtain shut, erasing everything.

4

Dusk.

Wearing her white hat, at the wheel of the Dodge, Mellie hums Nicole's rock tune to herself.

It is still raining. The car's headlights flash across pine trees, a downhill bend, grapevines, jumbled fragments of the road the young woman must take to get home.

Her house is a few kilometres from the village. Barely wide enough for two cars to pass abreast, the road winds up to the top of a hill overlooking Le Cap-des-Pins. There are a few villas scattered among the trees, but most of them have been closed up for the winter.

Without slowing down, Mellie Mau turns into a gravel drive, and with the confidence born of long habit, steers the car through a garden in which oleanders are still blooming, battered by the rain.

She stops with a great squeal of brakes in front of a white house – a rather sprawling, multi-level affair, with a roof of curved tiles.

Turning off her headlights, she picks up from the seat beside her a large *pain de campagne* and a clothing box with NICOLE emblazoned on it, then dashes the few steps to the house, slamming the car door behind her.

Shortly afterwards, a bedside lamp with a red shade is turned on.

It is Mellie Mau, entering her bedroom on the first floor. She has already taken off her hat, raincoat, and boots downstairs.

She opens the clothes box on her bed, unfolds her new dress, smoothens it out on the bedspread, and studies it thoughtfully, chewing on a thumbnail.

On the ground floor, a clock begins to strike seven.

At the second chime, Mellie turns and moves briskly across the room in her stockinged feet.

It is a room with several windows, cosy and feminine, decorated in white and pastel colours.

There are two large bedrooms on the first floor, separated by a shared bathroom.

At the final stroke of seven, Mellie is in front of the mirror over the bathroom sink, looking at her teeth.

She turns on the taps of the bath, tests the temperature of the water, takes a lipstick from a shelf, and enters the second bedroom, which belongs to her husband.

There are bookcases with their contents piled up in disorder, a huge map of the world covering one entire wall, sports trophies on top of a chest of drawers, university certificates in frames, and still more books – books everywhere.

An old pair of boxing gloves hangs from the upper-right corner of a large mirror, on which Mellie writes with her lipstick:

I'M FLAT BROKE

She returns immediately to her room. While the water gushes noisily into the bath, she goes back and forth from one bedroom to the other with the relaxed manner of a woman accustomed to living alone several days a week.

Standing beside her bed again, her skirt hitched up to her suspender belt, she undoes her stockings without bothering to sit down, gazing at her new dress the whole time. She hangs her stockings side-by-side over the endboard of the bed.

A moment later, she turns off the taps of the bath. She has put on a white towelling dressing gown.

As she carries her skirt and sweater into her bedroom, she piles her hair on top of her head and secures it with a comb. The only sound is the rattling of the rain against the window panes.

It is at this very moment, as she performs one of the most ordinary rituals of her sheltered life as a middle-class housewife – draping her skirt and sweater over the footboard – that Mellie Mau tumbles brutally into a different world.

For this ritual is interrupted by something incomprehensible: there had been two stockings on the footboard; now there is only one. Perplexed, Mellie picks that one up, looking for the other on the bedspread, then on the carpet by her feet. Almost doubting her own action of but a few seconds before, she turns around.

And a man is there, in front of her, with the missing stocking pulled down over his face.

She has not heard him enter the house, or her bedroom. He is suddenly and monstrously there, and his mask disguises nothing: it is the passenger from the bus.

Rigid with terror, Mellie cannot even summon the strength to scream.

Besides, the man does not leave her time to do anything. He attacks her the instant she sees him, in his sodden raincoat, a full head taller than she is. Incomprehensible.

She fights back when he grabs her; she tries to fend him off, to hit him, but it is a contest without cries, without words. There is only the sound of two people gasping for breath, and this panting makes their struggle even more frightening.

Yanking Mellie's dressing gown back from her shoulders with both hands, the man tries to pinion her arms behind her. Before he can do so, she manages to catch hold of the stocking stretched over his head, and the nylon rips open to reveal the face – the eyes – of a madman.

Pivoting slightly backwards, the stranger then punches her in the stomach with his right fist, with all his strength, as one would hit a man.

Bent double, the breath knocked clean out of her, Mellie finds herself dragged, thrown onto her bed, helpless. The rest is simply a nightmare – a stream of brief, incoherent, but precise images out of a nightmare.

Hunched over, her open mouth jammed into the pillow, Mellie tries desperately to breathe while the man's hands tear off her dressing gown.

With the belt from the gown, these hands tie her wrists together quickly, coldly, behind her back.

Mellie's eyes, wide with fear, stare through the open bathroom door at the light shining over the sink – quite close, blinding.

Raindrops pepper the bedroom windows, a solid, steady sound in the silence. Ten feet away from the windows, the man's raincoat lies on the carpet, with Mellie's comb flung on top of it.

With one hand, the man lying on Mellie grips her terrified face – tangled hair, laboured breathing – and forces her to look him in the eye.

The bedside lamp, tipped over on its table, projects the light from its naked bulb towards the bed – close, blinding.

The man's hand, clutching a fistful of Mellie's hair, pulls her head back, harder and harder, with studied brutality.

Her face twisted to one side, half unconscious from horror, Mellie is now no more than a doll without arms, without hands.

In her staring eyes, there is only that glare from the bare light bulb on the bedside table – close, blinding.

5

Utter darkness.

Then, slowly, Mellie's eyes open.

They open onto a window in the bedroom. The rain has stopped. Everything is peaceful. In the silence can be heard the ticking of a clock sitting on a bureau.

Mellie listens without moving.

She is lying on her side, sprawled across the bed, her hands untied, her new white dress draped over her naked body.

The house is absolutely quiet, except for the ticking of the clock.

She rolls onto her back, one forearm hiding her face. The belt from her dressing gown is still knotted around one wrist.

She undoes it in a kind of daze, picking at it with her teeth, since her fingernails are useless. She is withdrawn, inaccessible, shut out of her own life.

On her right leg she is wearing, unaccountably, one of her stockings. It is not attached to anything and has slipped down into bunched-up folds below her knee.

A moment – or an eternity – later, she steps cautiously out onto the landing. She is buttoning up her white dress, the closest thing at hand she found to put on.

She looks down the stairs.

She is not afraid; she can barely think.

She sees, from above, the front door open onto the soft breath of the night outside. Her white towelling dressing gown lies across the threshold.

In the front hall now, the young woman picks up her dressing gown, and at that moment her mind stops reeling.

She looks around, senses that she is alone in the house, that the man has gone. She closes the heavy door quickly, shooting all the bolts.

Mellie turns around with a start when the clock in the hallway strikes the half-hour. She looks at the clock face: half-past eight.

Her face haggard, the young woman makes her way through the whole of the ground floor, a blurry white universe with streaks of colour. As she walks by lamps she turns them on, one after another, and their light gleams on her quivering lips. She must do one thing: get to the telephone.

When she picks up the receiver and dials the operator, she is kneeling on a rug, beneath a big lamp, biting a nail on her left hand.

A ring, a click, a woman's voice: 'Yes?'

MELLIE: I ... I ... I want the police.

'What is your phone number?'

Mellie cannot remember anymore. She stares frantically into space, searching for it.

'Hello?'

MELLIE (*abruptly*): 18! It's 18, at Le Cap-des-Pins.

'Please hold.'

More noises on the line, another click. This time, a man's voice, impersonal, tired after hours on the job.

'Police station, how can I help you?'

Mellie does not answer. She has opened her mouth to speak. She raises a finger of her left hand to her mouth, then presses a very wide, flat wedding-ring of gold to her lips. She has not prepared her words beforehand, and how does one speak of such a thing?

On the other end of the line, patience is wearing thin.

'Hello? ... Hello! I'm listening!'

Mellie is unable to make a sound. Her wedding-ring clamped between her teeth, she imagines what would happen if she were to speak: she would be ashamed, her husband would be ashamed. She cannot.

'Hello! ... Who is this?'

Mellie hangs up. Timidly, as though she were the one to blame.

She stands up, takes a step, then another, realizing that she is acting like a guilty person – and the telephone rings, stridently, imperiously.

Mellie whirls around, and there is fresh anguish in her eyes: the police station is calling back, wanting to know what the hell she wanted.

Standing there, she hesitates for a long time, then reaches for the receiver.

The same woman's voice as before asks, 'Is this 18 at Le Cap-des-Pins?'

MELLIE: Yes.

'Did you reach the police station?'

MELLIE: Yes ... Yes, thank you.

'Please hold on – London is calling.' Then, through some interference on the line: 'Go ahead, London!'

There is silence again, then a man's voice, perfectly clear: 'Mellie?'

MELLIE (*relieved*): Tony? ... Is that you, Tony?

He gives a short, easy laugh. 'Of course it's me.'

MELLIE (*worried once more*): You're not coming home tonight?

TONY: Of course I am ... We're taking off in ten minutes. I'll be home at around eleven o'clock.

Silence.

TONY: Is something wrong?

Another silence. Mellie picks up the base of the telephone in her left hand, leans back against the wall. So many words are rushing into her head, she cannot manage to say any of them.

MELLIE: Oh, no ... Everything's fine.

TONY: Doesn't seem like it.

Still another silence. Then, a gleam of hope brightens the young woman's face.

MELLIE: Tony! Can I come and get you in the car at Marignane?

TONY: No ... A friend's bringing me back.

MELLIE: Oh, Tony ... Let me come!

TONY: I said no.

MELLIE: But why?

Another casual little laugh.

TONY: You drive like an idiot.

Mellie nods, disappointed, without answering.

TONY: Listen, sweetie ... I'm telling you, it's really not worth the trouble.

MELLIE: Come quickly.

TONY: You're angry?

MELLIE: No. Just come home quickly.

More silence.

TONY: See you soon, sweetie.

He has hung up. She stands still, with a stubborn ringing in her head. She feels like bursting into tears, but she does not cry. She never cries.

Staring down at the floor, she notices for the first time the nylon stocking she is wearing on her right leg, hanging down to her ankle. While setting the phone back in its place with one hand, she rips off the stocking with the other, the way one would wipe away dirt. She wads it up in her hand and throws it as hard and as far as she can across the room. She is in a living room painted white – a huge, empty room spread out on three different levels, broken up by flights of steps, decorated with heavy curtains and paintings in subdued colours, still largely unfurnished, yet gracious and lovely – after Mellie, the house is Tony Mau's only passion – but, well, it remains what it is: a huge, empty room.

A moment later, the blade of a large knife is thrust into the *pain de campagne* Mellie brought back from the village.

Mellie is in the kitchen, wearing her new dress half buttoned up, sitting against a wall, her bare feet braced on the tiled floor.

She is eating, gazing vacantly, surrounded by silence, eating like a child having a snack: a bit of bread, a nibble of chocolate.

She sees her reflection in a kitchen utensil hanging on a wall. With a forearm, she brushes a dangling lock of hair away from her temple.

And then, suddenly, with the bread almost at her lips, she freezes, alert, panic flooding back into her eyes. There was no noise, nothing. Or else, she's the only one who heard it.

She listens, holding her breath.

Silently, she puts down the bread and chocolate. She walks slowly from the kitchen, crosses the front hall and stands stock-still again, backed up against one of the living room walls.

The lamps are still on.

Mellie's eyes are riveted to a closed door straight in front of her. Without a sound, never taking her eyes from the door, she moves towards a rack holding several sporting guns. She takes down a double-barrelled shotgun – the one nearest to her – and opens a drawer in the chest beneath the rack. Feeling around inside it, she pulls out a box of cartridges.

She looks away from the closed door only to glance down at her hands, to see what she is doing.

The unopened box of cartridges is still wrapped in its cellophane, which Mellie tears off with her teeth. The sound rips through the silence of the house, quickening her terror.

No longer worried about being overheard, Mellie breaks open the gun and slips a fat red cartridge into each barrel.

She does this awkwardly because she has never done it before, has only seen her husband load the gun this way, but her shaking hands obey – the cartridges are of the correct gauge – she manages.

Snapping the stock back into place with a sharp clack, she stands paralysed with dread for two more seconds, staring at the closed door. And then, with surprising fury, she jumps at it, flings it open, screaming like an animal, because she cannot take any more of this fear, she has had enough of it all, she wants an end to it.

MELLIE (*shouting*): Come out of there!

Nothing, not a sound, except for the familiar hum of the central heating boiler. The open door reveals several steps leading down to a dark basement.

Mellie sweeps her hand across the light switch and leaps backwards.

No one. A bare light bulb below now illuminates the stairs, part of the basement, and at its far end, the garage and its large tip-up door, now closed.

A section of wall, however, cuts off the light on one side. Part of the basement remains in darkness.

Mellie waits, clutching the shotgun, looking down at this pocket of shadow. And then she speaks. Softly, all anger spent, in a voice that barely quavers.

MELLIE: Go away … I won't say anything to anyone … I won't press charges … Go away …

No movement in the basement. It is clear that the man has gone, that Mellie is talking to the air. Yet her voice grows more insistent.

MELLIE: You heard me on the telephone, I didn't say anything … No one will find out about it … (*louder*) Please, go away!

There is a noise in the darkness, the sound of someone who was sitting and who now stands up. And then, footsteps.

The man moves into the light, at the bottom of the stairs. He faces Mellie, in his raincoat, arms hanging at his sides, the way he appeared when he arrived in the village. He lifts towards her the same mute gaze, the same lifeless face.

He does not see the weapon pointed at him. He has eyes only

for those of the young woman, who tries not to flinch. And all of a sudden, he does something unbelievable: he has kept one of Mellie's stockings, and now he stretches it out in front of him. And he smiles. An ugly, satisfied smile.

Mellie fires, twice.

The first shot, full in the chest, punches the man towards the back of the garage. He is still standing, in the smoke from that blast, when he receives the second one, which flings him off to one side. He falls face down on the floor.

A dog barks in the distance.

Mellie is stupefied more than anything else. With eyes widened by a childlike incredulity, hardly frightened at all, she stares at the stranger lying down there beneath the bare light bulb.

She drops the gun instinctively, then tries clumsily to catch it, but it clatters down the steps.

Wearing the same look of disbelief, she goes down the stairs and over to the man sprawled in front of the entrance to the garage.

He is at her feet, struck down.

And suddenly, he moves. He looks up at her with a face that is crazed, distorted by rage, pain, or fear, or everything at once. His hand grabs with splayed-out fingers at the hem of her dress, takes hold of it.

Mellie lurches backwards without a cry, her mind numb with horror. She seizes the only weapon within reach: one of the oars of a rubber dinghy leaning against a wall of the garage. And she strikes, strikes with all her might, until her breathing is just sob after sob of loathing.

When the oar slips from her hands, she stops, looking like a wild woman.

She retreats, step by step, until her back hits the dinghy, which wobbles and comes tumbling down, taking her with it, along with all of everyday reality.

Then she springs to her feet, opens a door, and runs outside, into the night. She has only one idea: to flee as far from that place as she can.

Barefoot, dishevelled, her dress half-undone, she splashes through the puddles of rain, collapses against the door of the Dodge parked in front of the house, clambers in behind the wheel. Clapping her right hand over the ignition switch, she realizes that she does not have the key, that she must go back to look for it in the kitchen, in her bedroom, God knows where. In a panic, she looks at the lighted windows of the house. She cannot do it. She drops her head on the steering wheel, cradling her face in her arms, her whole body shivering like a sick animal.

She just sits there.

6

It is later, perhaps an hour later.

Mellie's hand picks up the lamp that was knocked over, stands it upright on the bedside table, takes up the bunch of keys she had left there.

She has put on her white raincoat and her boots. Her hair is combed, her movements are precise, her resolve is completely restored by the decision she has taken.

She straightens out the bedspread quickly, and throws all the things scattered across the carpet into a cupboard.

Backing towards the door, she glances around, checking to make sure the room looks tidy.

Down in the basement, the garage door is open.

The Dodge drives slowly into the garage. It stops a yard from the corpse. Mellie gets out and opens the boot of the station-wagon.

Without looking at him more than she has to, or giving in to her disgust, she takes hold of the man by his clothes and tries to drag him, to hoist him into the car. He is too heavy, too bulky for her ever to manage this. She straightens up, defeated but not discouraged, looking around for something that might help her.

She gets a tall wooden shutter that has been leaning against a wall and places it next to the body, which she rolls over onto the shutter.

There is blood on the floor where the man fell.

A few minutes later, on her knees, Mellie cleans these bloodstains with a floorcloth.

The man lies in the open boot of the Dodge. Only a single arm protrudes from beneath the piece of canvas now covering him.

The shutter is still propped up against the station-wagon. When she knocks it away, it falls flat against the concrete floor with a harsh, decisive bang.

7

The Dodge drives silently along the edge of the bay, which stretches for kilometres beyond Le Cap-des-Pins.

The road is empty, the night sky has cleared and is now sprinkled with stars, and across the bay gleam the myriad lights of the town of Le Lavandou.

At the wheel, Mellie hears only the crashing of the heavy waves upon the shore. She is watchful, her nerves on edge.

Coming to the end of the bay, taking a curve that hugs the shore, she receives a shock: dark forms loom ahead in a blaze of floodlights, with motorcycles on the shoulder, cars with whirling emergency lights parked sideways on the pavement – a police road block.

It is as though they were waiting for her.

The barricade appears so abruptly as she comes around the curve that she slams on the brakes, dazzled, and the station-wagon skids to a stop crosswise on the road.

A motorcycle policeman comes over to her, an ominous helmeted silhouette in the glare of the road block.

Her blood running cold, Mellie lowers her window. The man touches an index finger to his temple in salute.

'Driving licence and registration, please?'

Mellie opens her glove compartment. While she is looking for the documents, the policeman leans in at her window to check the inside of the vehicle.

In the boot, behind the two car seats, the dead wrist sticking out from under the canvas cover is wearing a watch with a round face and a metal band, and from quite close one can hear it ticking steadily, appallingly loud.

Another man calls out in a friendly voice.

'Is that you, Mellie?'

A different policeman – this one in plain clothes – approaches the Dodge. He touches the shoulder of the motorcycle policeman, who is trying to see beyond the back seat, and tells him, 'It's Madame Mau … I went to school with her husband.'

The motorcycle policeman moves away. The second man is about forty years old, well built, wearing a single-breasted raincoat. He, too, glances around inside the station-wagon.

'You're alone?'

Mellie has a lump in her throat and cannot bring herself to look the policeman in the face.

MELLIE: Good evening, Toussaint.

TOUSSAINT: And where are you off to like this?

A pause.

MELLIE: I'm picking Tony up from the airport.

Toussaint misinterprets Mellie's refusal to look up at him and fears he has annoyed her by questioning her too bluntly.

TOUSSAINT: The reason I'm asking is because we've been told to be on the lookout for an escapee … A mental patient. I wouldn't like you to have an unpleasant run-in with this character.

Mellie nods to show that she understands, but she cannot say a word.

TOUSSAINT: You didn't see anyone on the road?

Mellie shakes her head. She forces herself to look at the policeman. In the back of the station-wagon, the watch – its ticking now artificially loud – continues to live on a dead arm.

TOUSSAINT: Well, be careful … Good night, Mellie.

He walks off with the motorcycle policeman, raising his arm to tell the others to let the Dodge go on its way.

Mellie straightens up the car and drives slowly past the road block.

8

The boot of the Dodge is open.

Mellie pulls the dead body towards her until it falls to the ground, then she drags it with some difficulty across several yards of rocky terrain covered with stunted bushes.

She stops for a moment to catch her breath, to listen to the night. Something bright passes over her: the beam from a lighthouse.

The car is parked, with all its lights off, on a cliff surrounded by pine trees. On the other side of the bay, Le Lavandou can again be seen twinkling in the distance.

Mellie continues to drag the dead man, with stubborn, furious jerks, to the edge of the drop. There, with the lighthouse beam crossing and recrossing her panting face, she searches rapidly through the stranger's pockets, pulling out a few papers, a penknife, and a wallet. Then she removes his watch.

She wraps all of this up inside the piece of canvas that had covered him.

She acts quickly, not from fear of being seen, but in order not to see, or think.

Standing up straight again, she summons all her strength and pushes the man over into the void.

A dead weight in his unbuttoned raincoat, he falls some fifty metres and is swallowed up by the waves breaking at the foot of the cliff.

Then a man's voice is heard, shouting angrily and quite clearly.

'Mellie? Is that you, Mellie?'

9

S tartled, Mellie turns towards the voice with a muffled cry. She is in the semi-darkness of the basement, but a light bulb above her is suddenly turned on.

Standing at the top of the steps, framed in the doorway from the living room, is a man in shirt sleeves.

MELLIE: Yes, it's me.

She moves to the middle of the garage, in her white raincoat, with the canvas that had covered the dead man rolled up and tucked under her right arm.

The man upstairs is her husband.

He is livid.

TONY: Do you have any idea what time it is? … Where were you?

MELLIE: Tony, please!

TONY (*shouting louder*): Where were you?

Turning aside to hide her bundle, Mellie rids herself of it in the dark part of the basement. She comes forward to the bottom of the stairs, arms hanging at her sides.

TONY (*screaming*): Well?

MELLIE: I went to see Mummy.

For a second, Tony looks completely astonished. We can see him better now: he is a tall man with black hair, quite handsome, and extremely upset. He is thirty-five years old.

He raises his arms to heaven.

TONY: She went to see Mummy!

He repeats this sentence immediately in Italian, word for word, in the same tone. When he is angry, he repeats certain things like that in his native language, for emphasis.

At this moment, a woman appears next to him, in the doorway: it just happens to be Mellie's mother, Juliette.

There is silence at the top and bottom of the stairs. Breathing hard, Tony is too enraged to say a word. Mellie is speechless. As for Juliette, she sizes up the situation, but who knows what she thinks.

Tony turns abruptly on his heel and strides off towards the kitchen. After a moment, Juliette heaves a sigh of affected distress and follows her son-in-law.

Mellie climbs slowly up the steps.

Tony is seated at a table in the living room. In front of him sits what remains of the supper he prepared for himself. He is wearing navy-blue trousers, a white shirt, a black tie. A jacket bearing the insignia of Air France is hanging on the back of his chair.

He does not look at Mellie. He is still furious.

Not far from him, Juliette is sitting in an armchair. She lights a cigarette from the stub of the one she has just finished.

MELLIE (*softly*): I did go to Mummy's … I had trouble with the car.

TONY (*without turning around*): What kind of trouble?

MELLIE: The ignition.

TONY: You don't even know what the ignition is!

MELLIE: Another driver fixed the problem for me. He told me that's what it was.

TONY: Where was this?

MELLIE: On the road to La Madrague.

TONY: Your mother didn't see you on her way here!

JULIETTE (*calmly*): I didn't take that road.

Tony shrugs, says nothing more, and returns to his dinner. And then, abruptly, he shoves his plate away, he cannot help it, he starts up again.

TONY: As if that weren't enough, I, Tony Mau, had to make my own supper! (*He turns around to Mellie.*) You know what he would have done, my father, if my mother had gone out even once at this time of night? He would have shaken her silly!

He takes his head between his hands and says the same thing again in Italian.

TONY: I never saw my father do the cooking, or touch a single saucepan, or – I mean, I don't know!

Tongue-tied with anger, he looks around, sees a basket of eggs on the table, grabs one, and waves it under Mellie's nose.

TONY: An egg – you hear me? She would never have let him even break an egg! She would have been ashamed!

And he smashes the egg on the table. That calms him right down. He wipes his hand with his napkin, silent, a little embarrassed by his outburst.

JULIETTE: Your mother was a saint!

TONY: Exactly.

JULIETTE (*caustically*): Mellie wasn't that lucky.

Tony shrugs, watches his mother-in-law pick up her coat to leave; he is not a bit hostile – but he has no idea how to talk to Juliette. He looks over at Mellie, finally noticing that she is wearing a white cocktail dress.

TONY: That's your dress for tomorrow?

MELLIE (*caught off guard*): Yes … I wanted to show it to Mummy.

She looks at Juliette. Juliette looks at the dress. Silence.

MELLIE: What do you think?

JULIETTE: I think it's dirty.

There are indeed black smudges on the front of the dress, and it is all wrinkled.

MELLIE: I'll wash it, that's easy.

Juliette goes towards the door. On her way, she stubs out her cigarette in Tony's plate.

JULIETTE (*without turning around*): Plus, you've lost a button.

And she leaves.

Mellie, who lifts up the hem of her dress, and Tony, watching her, both realize that she has indeed lost a crystal button. Only the thread is left.

Mellie goes over to her husband, wraps her arms around him from behind, lays her head down on his shoulder. She is at the end of her tether; she cannot take any more.

We hear the sound of the front door closing behind Juliette.

Tony, without turning around, places one hand alongside his wife's face and draws it gently, tightly, against his own.

10

The white cocktail dress is on a hanger, spotless.

Mellie puts it up on a hook in the bathroom.

The door to her husband's room is ajar: through it she sees Tony in his bed, wearing burgundy pyjamas, leafing through a book and writing on a notepad.

She takes her white towelling dressing gown from the laundry basket, holds it rolled into a ball under one arm, and walks through her room out onto the landing. The door to Tony's room is open there, too.

TONY: Where're you going now?

MELLIE: To check on the boiler. I'm cold.

She goes downstairs. She is wearing a dressing gown of gleaming white silk with her initials, M. M., embroidered in blue over her heart.

In the basement, she opens the fire door on the boiler. She throws in her towelling dressing gown, the three broken pieces of the dinghy oar, the papers taken from the dead man's pocket, his penknife and the canvas cloth that had covered him.

She opens the wallet, but, in the end, she does not trouble to look inside it – or else she is sickened by the thought – and she tosses that into the flames as well.

She stands looking for a moment at the last object that reminds her of the horror of the evening: the dead man's wristwatch. An unusual-looking watch with a raised face, which continues its inexorable ticking.

She throws it into the fire.

There. Now the last link between her and the man she has killed is gone. Everything has been cleaned up. She will forget. Nothing has happened.

Wednesday, noon

11

Organ music.

Glittering candelabra are reflected in the glasses of the surpliced priest, who blesses the young couple as they exchange rings.

In the church the guests are standing up.

A hand touches the shoulder of a man in the last row to make him turn around.

Pointing to someone a few rows up in front, the hand gives him a Marseille newspaper – *Le Soir* – carefully folded to a front-page headline.

The newspaper moves from hand to hand until it reaches Tony Mau, who is wearing a dark suit; he takes the paper, somewhat surprised, and glances at it.

Next to him, in a coat and shawl of pale silk, Mellie takes a look, too; and her heart stops beating.

LE CAP-DES-PINS

BODY FOUND ON BEACH

Even though the incident happened where he lives, Tony Mau is not particularly interested. He simply hands back the newspaper with a fatalistic nod.

Mellie, however, cannot conceal her dismay. Luckily her husband turns back towards the altar and there is no one looking at her.

And yet there is.

As she glances around automatically, even before settling a safe expression on her face, her eyes meet those of a stranger who is standing near a pillar, both alert and amazingly at ease, watching her. He is dark, powerfully built beneath his navy-blue suit, with craggy features, a moustache, and the wary eyes of a big cat.

In spite of herself, Mellie looks for an instant into those eyes, which never leave her.

And then the man smiles at her – openly. A smile both warm and unsettling. If the tiger watching its doomed prey could wear a smile, it would be this one.

12

Crystal glasses filled with champagne are on a chased silver tray. When we next see this tray, which a waiter carries among the wedding guests, only two glasses remain upon it.

A man calmly picks them both up, one in each hand.

It is the stranger from the church. We are in the gardens of a grand hotel in Le Lavandou, with a view of the sea, in the sunshine of a fine afternoon. Gusts of music escape from behind the closed French windows of the hotel. There are many people outside, but it is Mellie Mau whom, from a distance, the man continues to watch.

In her white cocktail dress, with her golden hair, lovely and fragile at the same time, Mellie is standing near a tree, to one side.

The man moves towards her, threading his way placidly and easily through the crowd, holding the two glasses of champagne.

She glances around and sees him coming. Without hurrying, so as not to show that she is avoiding him, she crosses the terrace, where couples are waltzing.

She opens one of the French windows.

This door opens onto a simply furnished bedroom, in another time. On the rumpled bed, Juliette, naked in the arms of a lover, sits up suddenly with a look of anguish. Mellie, on the threshold, is a little girl of nine or ten with trembling lips and bewildered gaze, holding back her tears. Juliette, half hidden by her lover, cries out with pleading eyes, but we cannot hear the words – only the waltz.

And then, Mellie, in her white cocktail dress, has closed the French window behind her and is crossing what is only, after all, an empty lounge in the hotel.

When she opens another door, she finds the man she is trying to avoid waiting for her, all smiles.

He hands her a glass of champagne so naturally, with such quiet confidence, that she accepts it.

At first he just drinks from his own glass, without taking his eyes off her. When he speaks, his accent marks him as an American. He asks her only one question, but that one is a bombshell.

THE AMERICAN: Why did you kill him?

Mellie, who is sipping her champagne, freezes. She stares at him over the rim of her glass, astonishment battling with fear in her round eyes.

But behind that vulnerable appearance lies a quality one would never have suspected in her, something of which she herself has probably not been aware until yesterday's events: when she is in trouble, she reacts fast. Her look of dismay vanishes almost instantly.

MELLIE (*evenly*): What do I win, if I answer correctly?

The stranger's smile never wavers, and his attention to the young woman's reactions remains absolute.

THE AMERICAN: Nothing. But I win some time.

Mellie takes a sip of champagne, then makes a face.

MELLIE: It's not a very interesting game. Does it involve mathematics?

THE AMERICAN (*startled*): Involve *what*?

MELLIE: Mathematics. I'm unbeatable at maths.

They look at each other, without speaking. She cannot decide whether he is joking or not, but he can only have interpreted Mellie's fleeting confusion as astonishment.

As if in confirmation, he nods gently, as though accepting that this first round has been a tie.

He relieves the young woman of her glass, sets it down with his own on a small table. Then, with the same cool self-assurance, he takes Mellie in his arms for a dance. One does not refuse such an invitation at a wedding reception, and she allows herself to be persuaded.

A slow foxtrot has replaced the waltz.

As they dance, he keeps his left arm raised, holding his partner's hand. Which is how she receives her second shock: he is wearing a watch with a raised face and a metal band, identical to that worn by the passenger from the bus.

Luckily, the man's face is almost in profile beside hers, he is not looking at her, cannot see her inner turmoil – and she ducks her head closer to his shoulder to conceal her distress. But now a sound floats over the music of the orchestra: tick-tick, tick-tick ...

THE AMERICAN (*in a normal tone*): It's an American watch, that's all ... What did you think?

MELLIE (*same tone*): That you're an American, that's all.

THE AMERICAN: Americans scare you that much?

MELLIE: No. Watches do.

He sways his head slightly from side to side, dancing with her; she keeps her cheek close to his shoulder, and knows that nothing escapes him. The pair continue to chat in natural voices, like polite people.

MELLIE: Where do you come from?

THE AMERICAN: All over the place.

MELLIE: Why didn't you stay there?

THE AMERICAN: I followed that old adage: *cherchez la femme.*

The music stops. So do they, facing each other, and now Mellie must look him in the eye.

MELLIE: Are you a policeman?

He smiles even more broadly, shaking his head vigorously, as though that were the funniest thing in the world.

THE AMERICAN: Me? No!

MELLIE: Then you're out of luck, I've already got a man.

She is now looking in the direction of the French windows. The music begins again, but neither of them moves. Tony is out on the terrace, watching impassively. He may have been there for some time.

MELLIE: Excuse me, I must go.

The stranger, who is also looking at Tony, nods and allows the young woman to walk away.

A little later, in the gardens of the hotel, Tony and Mellie have taken leave of their hosts. Hand in hand, but with solemn faces, they reach the Dodge, which has been washed since the previous evening.

The American is leaning against the car, waiting for them.

His presence displeases both Mellie and Tony for different reasons, but he could not care less about that.

THE AMERICAN: I haven't got a car. I was told you might give me a lift.

TONY (*gruffly*): Where do you want a lift to? We're going to Le Cap-des-Pins.

THE AMERICAN: That's just where I'm going.

Relaxed smile, strong accent. He opens Mellie's car door for her.

When Tony gets in behind the wheel, with Mellie sitting beside him, the American is already ensconced in the middle of the back seat.

THE AMERICAN: My name is Dobbs. Harry Dobbs.

Tony glances at him in the rear-view mirror but does not reply. Neither does Mellie, whose eyes now glitter with anxiety.

The road runs alongside a vast beach that is almost deserted on this October afternoon. It is five o'clock, or perhaps later; the sun is sinking towards the horizon, dramatically backlighting the faces of the driver and passengers.

TONY: Have you been here long?

DOBBS: Since this morning.

TONY: Where are you staying?

DOBBS: At the Palm Hotel.

TONY: The Palm Hotel is closed.

DOBBS (*after a moment*): Not to me. I have a nice room, with lots of light, and red curtains.

He rests his elbows nonchalantly on the back of their seat. He seems quite satisfied with life.

Now they're on the main road leading to Le Cap-des-Pins.

TONY: You're here on business?

DOBBS: You could say that.

TONY: What kind of business?

DOBBS: Hunting.

The American's face is turned towards Mellie; he looks her up and down casually. She stares straight ahead at the road.

TONY: There's no hunting around here.

DOBBS: That depends on what you're hunting.

While driving, Tony shoots him a look in the rear-view mirror. He misunderstands the way the American is looking at his wife and what the man meant by that last remark.

Tony looks over at Mellie and notices that because of the missing button, the bottom of her dress hangs open more than it should, leaving her legs uncovered well above the knees.

TONY (*to his wife*): You haven't found that button you lost?

Mellie senses the reproach hidden in his question and pulls down the hem of her dress. But if she is uneasy, it is not because of that.

MELLIE: I'll ask Nicole.

She does not want to look at the stranger leaning between her and Tony. And then, she cannot help herself.

As she expected, his cat's eyes rove from the bottom of her dress to her face, taking in everything. But his smile is so calm that this business of the lost button probably means nothing to him.

The station-wagon arrives at the point where the narrow road into the village branches from the main road. Tony stops the car abruptly and turns around to Dobbs.

TONY: Here you are.

The stranger does not protest. He opens his car door and steps out. He looks up and down the road.

DOBBS: The Palm Hotel is still quite a way from here!

TONY (*curtly*): We're going in this direction.

And as soon as the car door is closed, he drives off.

Dobbs watches the car disappear, still with that air of being perfectly pleased with life. And then, absently, his right hand pulls on one of the buttons of his jacket, as though testing the strength of the thread.

13

Wearing only his pyjama bottoms – the same ones as the night before – Tony sits on the edge of his bed, counting out five hundred-franc notes. There are several stacks of them.

He turns his head when he hears Mellie enter the room, wearing a white house-dress with the initials M. M. on the breast pocket. In her arms she carries three of Tony's shirts, freshly ironed.

TONY: Come here, sweetie.

Mellie packs the three shirts into a small suitcase lying open on a table, picks up a lighted cigarette from the ashtray next to the suitcase, and goes over to her husband.

She places the cigarette between his lips. In return he gives her some money, nodding at the mirror where she had written in lipstick:

I'M FLAT BROKE

Mellie turns around, sees the message. For a few seconds, she is suddenly taken back to the previous day, to her previous life.

TONY: It's not enough?

MELLIE: It's plenty.

She is standing in front of him. With his cigarette in his mouth, one eye half-closed because of the smoke, he snaps a rubber band around the rest of the money.

MELLIE: When will you be back, Tony?

TONY: Saturday noon.

He tosses the roll of notes into his suitcase and stands up. He is tall and thin, with a dark, handsome face.

MELLIE: You're taking a lot of money with you.

TONY: That's my business.

Something is worrying him, too. He goes to the bathroom without looking at Mellie. He rummages in a cupboard.

Mellie has gone over to the huge map of the world that covers the wall. Little blue aeroplanes are attached to it with magnets, clustered around Marseille.

MELLIE: Tony, where're you going?

TONY: Djibouti.

She moves an aeroplane down the map to Africa. She chews a nail on her left hand.

MELLIE: After that?

TONY (*coming back into the room*): Cairo and Rome.

He throws an electric razor into his suitcase, adds a few wash things. Mellie moves two more little planes across the wall map.

MELLIE: What's it like, Djibouti?

TONY (*shrugging*): Like all the rest.

She looks at him. He turns his back on her.

MELLIE (*softly*): What's the matter, Tony?

TONY (*without looking at her*): The guy who helped you get the car started, last night – was it Harry Dobbs?

He says that in a voice so tense, so low, that at first the young woman does not understand.

MELLIE: Who?

TONY (*turning around*): The American!

Mellie shakes her head, several times, torn between amazement and the desire to confess that she lied the night before, that his suspicion is off the mark, that it is all much more serious.

TONY: You'd never met him before?

She shakes her head again, sharply. He stares at her in silence, sombrely, gnawed at by something beyond his control; and then he accepts her denial, he believes her. He has never known her to lie.

MELLIE (*discouraged*): Why are you being like this, Tony? …
Why are you jealous?

TONY: A man who isn't jealous isn't a man.

He opens a cupboard and reaches in for an Air France uniform,
which he leaves hanging on the pole, as he tries to master this thing
that is eating him alive.

MELLIE: What have I done now?

TONY: I saw you dancing with him!

He turns back to her, and his tall body, his voice, his black eyes
radiate an angry energy that transforms him with astonishing
speed. He points his finger at her, marking his words.

TONY: You know what my father used to tell my mother? (*He
lowers his voice.*) 'If someone looks at you, you'll tell me! If someone
touches you, I'll kill him!'

Then he sees Mellie as she really is – petrified. His fury melts
away.

He takes his Air France uniform out of the cupboard, checks
the pockets automatically. Off in the distance, police sirens can be
heard.

MELLIE (*quietly*): I'll never dance with anyone else again, I
promise you.

TONY: Fine.

MELLIE: I'd like to drive you to the airport tomorrow morning.

TONY: Fine.

He tosses the uniform on the bed and takes her in his arms. He
hugs her without saying anything.

Their silence is broken by the distant sirens, which are coming
closer.

Mellie turns her head lightly against her husband's chest, to
listen. There is fear in her eyes again. She hugs her husband tighter.

And the sirens fade away.

Thursday, 10.30 a.m.

14

L e Lavandou.
  Mellie has just bought some papers at a newspaper kiosk. She walks back to the Dodge, which is parked in a little square drenched in sunshine, slashed by harsh shadows.

It seems like summer again.

The car door hangs open; Mellie sits sideways on the seat, behind the steering wheel. She is wearing a skirt, a white jacket, and has a sky-blue silk scarf knotted loosely around her neck.

She folds up the newspaper she has been reading, tosses it aside, and opens another one immediately.

She has bought four local papers. This one, *Le Méridional*, is the last. She scans the pages from top to bottom, turning them nervously. It is obvious that she has not found what she is looking for.

She hurriedly gathers up the newspapers. After a moment's thought, she throws the useless papers away in a dustbin and crosses one of the narrow, bustling streets leading down to the harbour. She is carrying an empty shopping basket. She stops suddenly in front of a gunsmith's. There is a row of shotguns in the window display. Below them sit boxes of cartridges, flat on their sides.

Mellie stares through the glass at one of these cellophane-wrapped boxes. It looks just like the one she opened to kill the passenger from the bus.

15

With her shopping basket now full of provisions sitting on the seat beside her, Mellie drives past her mother's bowling alley. She notices that one of the door shutters is open; that lights are on inside.

She parks the Dodge in the lay-by at the edge of the beach. As she walks towards the concrete building, children shout and play ball all around her.

Cutting short the cries from outside, a large black ball smashes into the pins at the end of a lane and tips all ten of them over in a clean strike.

Alone in the deserted amusement hall, the bowler, Harry Dobbs, turns for a second to the door that has just opened. Then he picks up another ball and pays no further attention to Mellie Mau.

She hesitates on the threshold, rather taken aback to find him there – and yet not so surprised, after all, for somehow she knew he would be waiting for her.

He has taken off his jacket. He is wearing a white shirt, the collar unbuttoned. There is only one word for him: brute.

As he rolls the ball, she closes the door and walks towards him, past the pin-setting machinery of the bowling lanes, illuminated by the spotlights over the miniature car racetrack.

There is another crash of overturned pins.

DOBBS (*without looking at her*): How much will you bet that I'll beat you?

MELLIE: I don't know how to bowl.

Dobbs turns to face her. And then he goes over to his jacket, which he has draped over the back of a chair, and feels around inside a pocket.

DOBBS: Who's talking about bowling?

MELLIE: How did you get in?

Dobbs points vaguely in the direction of the pin-setter.

DOBBS: Through the door.

He has retrieved a cigarette from his jacket. He lights it.

DOBBS: I went to your house first, but you weren't there.

He comes back over to Mellie. She looks at him, without saying a word.

DOBBS: I know where you were. At Marignane. You went to the airport with your husband.

He picks up the ball waiting for him at the end of the return chute by the bowling lane.

DOBBS: It took you an extra three-quarters of an hour to get back, but I know the reason for that, too. You read all the newspapers.

He turns to look at her, adjusting his grip on the ball.

DOBBS: Unfortunately, the papers haven't said anything more about the body found yesterday morning.

Mellie is still silent. Her heart could explode, now, but nothing will show on her face.

He lets go of his ball and it rolls, rolls, knocks over the pins with another crash.

MELLIE (*quietly*): What do you want from me?

DOBBS (*as though nothing could be more obvious*): A little chat.

MELLIE: We've already said everything we have to say to each other, yesterday, at the wedding.

DOBBS: Yesterday I still hadn't seen your house. (*A pause.*) Very nice house. Your husband's a pilot for Air France, I believe?

MELLIE: A navigator.

Sitting down on the ball return chute, Dobbs smokes his cigarette.

DOBBS: A navigator must earn quite a bit of money. About how much?

MELLIE (*curtly*): What do you want to talk to me about?

He points to the far end of the room, to the glazed door facing the beach.

DOBBS: The man you saw ride into town on the bus.

For an instant, they are both silent. Then Mellie shakes her head and begins to speak, only to be cut off.

DOBBS: Your mother told me that.

MELLIE: It's true, I did see a stranger get off the bus. So what? I hardly noticed him.

DOBBS: You saw him again later on.

MELLIE: That's not true.

Dobbs stands up and throws his cigarette away from him, speaking faster, louder, pointing his whole arm towards the other end of the village.

DOBBS: You took off your clothes to try on a dress in a shop, and he was on the pavement, outside the shop window, watching you … A voyeur!

Mellie is struck dumb. She shakes her head again, slowly, but not to deny anything – she does not understand how he has found all this out. The explanation follows immediately.

DOBBS: It was your friend Nicole who told me that.

He is quite composed once more, perfectly relaxed. He is running this show – and he knows it. He collects a ball from the return chute.

MELLIE: You know Nicole?

DOBBS (*without turning around*): I've met lots of people since I arrived here.

He prepares to bowl the ball.

MELLIE: You told me you weren't with the police. Why are you interested in this man?

Instead of releasing the ball, Dobbs hangs onto it at the last moment, but he does not turn around. He just pauses in mid-motion.

DOBBS: *You* told *me* you were good at mathematics. This man is interesting.

And then he bowls the ball, off it goes, and as it rolls down the wooden lane, Mellie has already started to reply, raising her voice, too, determined not to let him get the better of her.

MELLIE: Not to me he isn't! I didn't know he was going to get killed! Or that someone was going to come asking me a lot of questions! Or anything!

The ball mows down the ten pins with a shattering noise that imposes silence. Dobbs does not move. He stands there in his white shirt and navy-blue trousers, staring into space.

If Mellie could see his face, she would understand that she has walked right into his trap, that he does not believe his luck to have scored this unexpected point. But she cannot see his face. Slowly, he turns around. He is not smiling. He looks at her with something new in his eyes – a kind of friendly understanding – and then, he slips back into character, heaves a deep sigh.

DOBBS: That's true. (*Silence.*) But give it a try. When he was spying on you, out in front of the shop, what did he have in his hands?

And he shows her his own empty hands. Mellie looks at them coldly, silently, but when she looks up again …

The passenger from the bus is at the shop window, motionless, with rain streaming down his face. He is gazing at her, and she, standing there undressed in the changing cubicle, is staring back at him, fascinated. He holds his red bag in his arms, and she suddenly sees this bag close-up, filling the vision she has of this moment.

Mellie shakes her head gently, like someone who does not remember, but it is the other way round: she recalls this red bag, which the man no longer had at the time of the murder, with such brutal clarity that she feels stunned.

DOBBS: You know perfectly well what he was holding – you tell one lie after another.

He goes over to the return chute to pick up a ball, and when Mellie does not reply, he glances at her. Then he notices a fixed look on her face and realizes that she is truly bewildered.

His craggy features register his dawning comprehension.

DOBBS (*surprised by his discovery*): You really forgot about the bag! You have no idea what happened to it!

Mellie pulls herself together. She unties the scarf knotted around her neck, both to disguise her dismay and because she feels her face flushing hotly.

MELLIE: Why should I? I couldn't care less about that man!

DOBBS (*louder than Mellie*): You're the last person who saw him! I've questioned the entire village!

MELLIE (*even louder than Dobbs*): So what!

She has nothing but her scarf to throw at his head, but she throws it anyway, with pathetic rage. He catches it in the air with one hand, coolly inhales its scent, folds it, and holds it out to her. When she does not take it back, he lets it fall to the floor.

DOBBS: There's only one explanation: you brought him home with you in your car.

Mellie finds Dobbs's idea so unlikely that she sniggers in response. The two of them have calmed down: Dobbs, because he has come to the end of what he knows; Mellie, because she realizes this from his one step too far.

DOBBS: No one can move about around here without a car.

MELLIE (*acidly*): You manage!

DOBBS: I've got one.

He turns the bowling ball over and over in his hands. Mellie darts a glance back at the door.

MELLIE: You didn't have one yesterday afternoon.

DOBBS (*correcting her*): I *said* I didn't have one.

Mellie marches angrily past the pin-setting machinery to the door and flings it open onto the bright sunshine outside.

DOBBS (*behind her*): The red one. I just love red!

She sees that at the end of the little street overlooking the beach, there is indeed a red Ford Mustang parked by the side of the road.

She whips around, leaving the door open, and dashes over to the bar.

Dobbs, who was preparing to bowl another ball, calmly watches her rush past him.

She flicks a switch behind the counter and the bowling lanes go dark.

DOBBS (*protesting*): Hey! I've paid my money!

MELLIE: I'm giving it back!

Going over to him, she fumbles nervously in a pocket of her jacket, pulling out notes and coins. In her hurry, she drops the coin she had intended to give him.

She bends down to pick it up.

Then something rather pitiful happens which Dobbs watches in silence: she cannot pick up the coin because her fingernails are bitten to the quick.

She keeps trying, and, in her frustration, she slides the coin along the smooth floor, trying to find an uneven spot that will allow her to grip the coin by its edge.

Dobbs bends down and picks it up.

For a second, their heads are quite close together. On Dobbs's face, we see once more that look of understanding, that fleeting air of kindness. On Mellie's, the realization of her own helplessness. Of her inability not only to pick up a fallen coin, but to defend herself against Dobbs.

They straighten up at the same moment.

MELLIE: Get out.

He nods, slips the coin into his pocket, and sits down to remove the bowling shoes he has been wearing and put his own back on.

DOBBS (*deliberately*): I'm going to find that red bag, Mellie … There aren't that many places where he could have stashed it. If it isn't at your house, then he must have checked it in at the station.

MELLIE: Leave me alone.

He walks over to the open door, putting on his jacket as he goes. Before he leaves, he gives her one of his feline looks, watchful, surer of himself than ever.

DOBBS: Not until I've got that bag. Not for a single minute. And believe me, Mellie, it would be better for you if I find it before the police do.

She remains still for only an instant after he has gone, whereupon she runs to the door and closes it behind him.

Then she retrieves her silk scarf hastily from the floor, turns out the lights over the electric racetrack and runs to the entrance facing the beach.

On opening the door, she finds three policemen waiting in front of it.

She is so startled that she steps back.

Toussaint – the police inspector in plain clothes she saw on the night of the murder – is there with two uniformed officers.

TOUSSAINT: You're leaving, Mellie?

She nods. The shouts of the children playing across the street are audible again.

TOUSSAINT: I saw your car parked outside. I had something I wanted to ask you.

He seems apprehensive. As he moves forward, she steps further back, and he comes into the room. Alone. He closes the door on the other two policemen.

He looks around without saying anything.

MELLIE: Yes, Toussaint?

She has her heart in her mouth and is trying desperately to hide her distress.

TOUSSAINT: Well, here's the thing. It's about the poker game we're supposed to have Saturday, when Tony gets back … Over at your house …

She looks at him, with no idea what he is talking about, but she is already breathing more easily. He has not come to talk to her about the murder.

TOUSSAINT (*more and more embarrassed*): I've been losing a lot this Autumn, Mellie … I'd rather speak to you about it, because Tony will listen to you … And then, you're easier to talk to … Anyway, I'll need a small loan …

For one second, Mellie could shout with joy, she is so relieved.

TOUSSAINT: Of course, that's if Tony doesn't mind … I don't want to be any trouble.

MELLIE (*hurriedly*): Not at all! I'll tell him, I'm sure he'll say yes!

The inspector's relief is almost as great as her own. More than pleased to have got through this humiliating experience, he already has his hand on the doorknob.

TOUSSAINT: Thanks, Mellie.

Outside, the two officers are waiting in a police car parked a few yards from Mellie's Dodge, in the lay-by along the shore.

A noontime silence now reigns on the beach.

Mellie and Toussaint cross the road, walking towards Mellie's car.

TOUSSAINT (*suddenly*): You know, the man who was found dead early yesterday morning, he was a boxer. Bruno Sacchi.

Mellie has her guard up once more, and does not reply.

TOUSSAINT: You hadn't heard?

MELLIE: I saw yesterday's paper. There was nothing in today's.

She gets into her car.

TOUSSAINT (*leaning in at her window*): Well, that's orders from on high! Not another word is to appear in print until they've arrested the guilty woman.

Try as she might to seem natural, Mellie cannot keep from looking up at him in wide-eyed surprise.

MELLIE: The guilty *woman*?

TOUSSAINT (*smiling*): Yes. They already know it was a woman who did it.

He shakes Mellie's hand without noticing the change in her expression.

TOUSSAINT: It's amazing how much they can find out! Well, see you on Saturday, Mellie! … And thank you!

He walks off to the patrol car. She sits motionless in the driver's seat, unable even to say goodbye.

16

The front wheels of the Dodge swing up to the house and brake suddenly in a spray of gravel.

Mellie gets out and takes a few steps, carrying her shopping basket. And then she stops, looking up at the windows.

She sees that image again: the bus passenger's red bag, in the rain.

In the sunshine, Mellie runs around the side of the house. Breathless, she hoists open the garage door in one great heave.

She bends down beneath a workbench and lifts up a heavy locker lid that slams noisily to the floor.

The bag is not there.

She rushes over to a tool cupboard, finds nothing, dashes to the rubber dinghy leaning against the wall and tips it over. Nothing there either.

She catches her breath, then turns around abruptly, looking desperately about her for the red bag.

Not long afterwards, she is in Le Cap-des-Pins, in front of the glazed doors of the little railway station, a building with white walls and blue shutters.

She peers inside through one of the glass panes in the door and sees the red bag at the far end of the lobby, sitting on a shelf along with other things in the left-luggage room: an ordinary airline bag, so near, so inaccessible. A train thunders through the station without stopping.

The rattling din has not yet died away when Mellie enters the waiting room, nervous and alert.

It is deserted, but, framed in another doorway wide open onto the platform, two station employees stand talking with their backs to Mellie.

She hears one of them speaking in a tone of exasperation.

'Everybody lies! Listen, when I'm talking, I never know if I really mean what I say!'

Turning towards the ticket window, Mellie hesitates. And then, why not, she goes for it.

Only a few steps bring her to the left-luggage room, where she snatches the red bag from behind the counter; a few more steps and she is back in the lobby; yet another few will carry her on outside, her heart thudding like a jackhammer.

Still afraid that one of the two employees will turn around, she keeps her eyes fixed on the door to the platform as she backs out of the station entrance – and bumps into a man waiting on the threshold behind her.

Whirling around, she is so astonished that she lets out a muffled cry.

It is Harry Dobbs, standing absolutely still, shoulders square in his tweed jacket, looking happier than ever with life and even, for once, openly and mockingly triumphant.

He looks at the red bag, then at Mellie, and heaves a little sigh.

She is aghast to find herself in front of him like this – and holding the bag, which is like a confession – but her reaction is astounding.

MELLIE (*with deep relief*): Ah! I was just about to come and look for you!

Dobbs has seen everything, so he takes this in his stride, but his smile vanishes instantly.

DOBBS: You're kidding, right?

MELLIE (*evenly*): You told me you'd leave me alone when you got your hands on this bag. So, here it is!

And she tosses it into his arms.

She tries to walk off.

He grabs the young woman by the elbow and shoves her back against the station door.

He unzips the red bag, rummages quickly through its contents. His face tells her right away that this is not what he expected: two dirty shirts, some papers, a toothbrush, and nothing more.

He goes through the papers anyway. He stops, turns something over. He looks up at Mellie with those cat's eyes of his.

He is a little surprised, but there is something else as well; and she knows before he opens his mouth that he has just won the next round.

DOBBS: I can't leave you alone, not now.

He holds the paper out to her. It is a 5 × 7" photograph, and on the back of it is an address, written by hand.

TONY MAU

CHEMIN DE LA ROCADE

LE CAP-DES-PINS (VAR)

She turns it over to look at the photograph and sees a half-length shot of Tony, in an Air France uniform. He is obviously unaware of the camera.

She stands there in silence, dazed.

DOBBS (*softly*): Isn't that your address?

She nods. He retrieves the picture from her hands, but she hardly notices. She looks up at him with eyes that do not understand, that beg for an explanation.

DOBBS (*still softly*): The owner of this bag went to your house, Mellie.

MELLIE: That's not true!

She tears the bag away from him and races to her car. Distraught, she gets behind the wheel, only to find that her keys are not hanging from the ignition. When she looks over at Dobbs, she knows that there is no point in searching for them.

He comes over to her, with that fluid, nonchalant walk of his, jingling the little bunch of keys between his thumb and forefinger.

She crosses her arms in front of the steering wheel and stares at the windscreen, trying to collect her thoughts.

She does not look at him when he leans in at the open car window. With the hand holding the keys, he gestures for her to give him back the bag. They make the exchange.

MELLIE: Give me that picture!

He shakes his head, sorry, no.

DOBBS: It's worth a lot of money to me, Mellie.

Contemplating the stubborn profile of the unhappy young woman, Dobbs seems reluctant to press his advantage. After a glance at his American watch, he sighs.

DOBBS: I'm hungry. Lunch is on you.

17

Four eggs sizzle in a frying pan.

Mellie lifts the pan off the gas-ring and slides the eggs onto a plate, which she places in front of Harry Dobbs.

He is sitting at the round table in her kitchen, just finishing a salad. He picks up a large glass of milk.

DOBBS: You're not eating?

Mellie shakes her head. Over her blouse and white skirt she is wearing a little apron embroidered with big letters that spell out: LOVE LOVE.

She takes a bottle from the fridge and pours ketchup all over the fried eggs. Dobbs watches her in some perplexity.

DOBBS: Is that for me?

MELLIE (*confidently*): Americans live on ketchup and milk. I'm unbeatable at geography.

He pushes his plate away, without comment.

DOBBS: Mellie, that's short for what?

MELLIE: Mélancolie.

She smiles at his astonishment. This is the first real smile she has given him. She draws up a chair and sits down next to him.

MELLIE (*brightening*): They were going to call me Mélanie, it was my grandmother's name. But it was my father who went to the registry office. At the last moment he told the guy at the desk, 'No, no, not Mélanie, don't write down Mélanie!' Except, well, the clerk had already started to write! … You follow me?

Dobbs nods, as serious as can be.

They stare at each other so fixedly that Mellie cannot carry it off, and her smile fades.

MELLIE (*in a lower voice*): So they wouldn't have to cross anything out, they named me Mélancolie ... Eat, it's going to get cold.

DOBBS (*after a while*): I like your father.

MELLIE: He left when I was nine. He never came back.

Dobbs nods, as though in commiseration.

DOBBS: And that, what is it?

He points to the words LOVE LOVE embroidered on the young woman's apron.

MELLIE: A present. Some friends of Tony's, in Hong Kong, or God knows where.

Dobbs drinks the last of his glass of milk with a preoccupied air, as if he were pondering what she has just told him.

DOBBS: Tony must have friends all over the place, right?

The truce is over. We can tell from the sound of his voice, but also from Mellie's face, because she is suddenly wary. She does not answer.

DOBBS: When was this picture taken, Love Love?

MELLIE: Let me see it, I'll tell you.

He produces the photograph from one of his jacket pockets and shows it to her again. Her hand darts across the table to snatch it, but he has anticipated this and whisks it away.

DOBBS (*reprovingly*): Love Love!

MELLIE (*reluctantly*): I think it was last year.

Dobbs slips the photograph back into his pocket.

MELLIE (*raising her voice*): But that doesn't mean Tony knew this Bruno Sacchi!

DOBBS: Well, you know his name, in any case.

MELLIE: Someone told me a little while ago!

DOBBS (*leaning his elbows on the table*): I'm sure that he cannot have known your husband. Otherwise, he wouldn't have needed a photograph to recognize him.

MELLIE (*delighted*): There – now that's psychology.

DOBBS: I'm unbeatable at psychology. (*Dobbs eats from a cup of yogurt with a spoon.*) Only, in certain businesses, people don't need to know one another. And no one is any the wiser, it's perfect!

Mellie's mouth has gone dry again, and she shakes her head. Dobbs takes no notice.

DOBBS: Sacchi came here on Tuesday evening on business, not by accident. Whatever happened, when he found you alone in the house, that's for you to tell me.

She gives him an icy look.

MELLIE (*curtly*): Do you want some coffee before you leave?

DOBBS: I have no intention of leaving. (*Smiling.*) Besides, I'm not in any hurry.

MELLIE (*appalled*): You can't be thinking I'm going to let you stay here?

DOBBS (*affably*): Where do you expect me to go? To the police?

He leans back in his chair and flashes at a speechless Mellie the same smile she saw in the church: warm, sympathetic, yet terribly disquieting. This smile is immediately followed by a struggle that is silent and absolutely futile. Dobbs has thrown Mellie into an armchair, pinning her down so firmly that she cannot move. Thrusting the rim of a glass full of spirits between her teeth, he forces her to drink.

About fifteen minutes have passed, or perhaps half an hour.

Mellie tries desperately to turn her head away, but Dobbs holds her tightly; she is choking, she swallows mouthfuls and coughs, the alcohol runs out of the corners of her mouth, and he does not let go of her until she has finished the glass.

He seems to have gone raving mad.

Breathless, crazed with anger and disgust, Mellie wipes her mouth furiously with her forearm.

Dobbs is standing in front of her, holding the empty glass in one hand. With the other, he snatches up an open bottle of whisky sitting on a low table.

77

She tries to get up, but all he takes is one step forward and she collapses back into the chair.

For one moment, in that long, spacious living room, there is no sound besides the young woman's rapid breathing. Mellie and Dobbs are at the far end of the room. The large stone fireplace opposite the sofa is cold and empty.

Mellie looks up at Dobbs with a kind of defiance, and tosses her head.

She brushes off her blouse, smooths her hair, then turns her head sharply towards him as she hears the gurgle of whisky flowing into a glass.

He is pouring her another drink.

He leans forward to give it to her.

MELLIE (*pleadingly*): But why are you doing this?

DOBBS: It's my job.

MELLIE (*pulling herself together*): Where will it get you when I start seeing two, or three, or even four Mr Dobbses?

DOBBS: You'll pick one of them to hear your confession, Love Love.

He holds the full glass out to her. She stares at it but draws back, horrified, shaking her head.

MELLIE: If I scream, there are people in the house up the hill, they'll hear me.

DOBBS (*with a gesture of indifference*): Fine.

She hesitates, looking from Dobbs to the full glass. She closes her eyes, puts her fingers in her ears, and lets out a shriek. She is not putting her heart into it, however, and stops of her own accord.

DOBBS: I checked this morning. There's no one at home. Like on Tuesday evening, when you killed him.

MELLIE (*evenly*): That's not true!

Dobbs waggles his arm over the chair to show that he is tired of holding out the glass.

MELLIE: I won't drink it.

DOBBS (*cynically*): Who's asking you to drink? Tell me what happened on Tuesday evening instead. (*He waits.*) Drink – I hate repeating myself!

She reaches out cautiously for the glass. Head hanging, she looks at the amber liquid held close against her chest. And then abruptly, with a vicious look, she throws this liquid at Dobbs's face.

He is beginning to know her and ducks to one side, untouched. But he is furious. He grabs the empty glass from her and fills it again.

DOBBS: If you do that once more, even once more, I'll spank you!

Mellie gives a strange little laugh. Nervous laughter, but laughter all the same. Probably at the unusual threat he has just made.

MELLIE: You'll what?

Dobbs explains deliberately, emphatically.

DOBBS: I'll put you across my knee, pull down your pants, and give you a good spanking!

She looks into his eyes, and he is so clearly prepared to carry out his threat that she turns away.

Dobbs holds out the brimming glass again.

She takes it and drinks without looking at him, gulp after gulp, trapped in her armchair.

DOBBS: All of it!

She drinks it all. He takes the glass back and walks away from her.

He has recovered his good humour, and gazes around the living room with appreciation.

DOBBS: Pretty fancy. Tony sure knows how to get what he wants.

He puts the glass back on the low table and goes to stand in front of the French windows, looking out.

DOBBS: Sailors and flyboys, they have the good life. A woman in every port, a racket in every airport.

Already struggling against the soporific effect of the alcohol, the young woman refuses to be intimidated by his insinuation.

MELLIE: I know Tony.

DOBBS (*turning around*): And I know Sacchi.

He walks slowly back to her.

DOBBS: Well? Ask me to tell you about him!

MELLIE: It'll make you thirsty.

Ignoring her jibe, Dobbs leans down to the young woman until their faces are so close they almost touch.

DOBBS: He was a very interesting case for a psychiatrist: a liar, a thief, a sadist, and a sex maniac.

He takes something from his pocket and tosses it up and down in his hand: a walnut.

DOBBS: He did have his good points, though. Walnuts, for example …

He grips Mellie by one wrist and drags her after him so that they are both facing the French windows in the living room.

DOBBS: He taught me something about walnuts.

She is puzzled. He then does something unexpected with incredible speed and violence: using all his strength, he throws the walnut at one of the French windows. We hear a loud crack, but the glass does not break – it is the nut that splits open and falls in two onto the carpet.

Mellie starts back. Dobbs quietly picks up the two pieces.

DOBBS: Try it.

He pulls another walnut from his pocket and puts it in Mellie's hand. She stands there, baffled, staring at the glass door in front of her.

DOBBS (*encouraging*): Throw hard!

She looks at him. He is eating the kernel, and waiting. There is no mockery in his expression. He is probably thinking that she would never dare …

And that is what does it: she cocks her arm and hurls the nut as hard as she can against the windows. A pane of glass shatters into smithereens that shower to the floor with a dreadful crash.

The two of them contemplate the mess silently, impassively. Then Dobbs nods his head.

DOBBS: You're in love … When it's the glass that breaks, it means you're in love.

MELLIE (*exasperated*): Get out! I know Tony has nothing to do with Sacchis and Harry Dobbses! … You know what it's called, what you're doing?

DOBBS (*pretending to be contrite*): Concealing evidence.

MELLIE (*convincing herself*): Blackmail! I'm the one who should call the police! You hear me? I want to go to the police! Yes! … I want to go to the police.

As she speaks she takes off her apron and tosses it aside.

Dobbs looks her up and down. And then, with no more ado, he grabs her by one arm and pulls her roughly towards the front door.

Along the way he collects the young woman's jacket from the back of an armchair and throws it in her face. She loses a shoe with a one-inch heel as they clatter down the front steps, but he just picks it up and takes it with him, hauling Mellie along behind him.

18

The Dodge drives along the only street in the village.

Dobbs, who is at the wheel, stops on the esplanade overlooking the beach, not far from Nicole's boutique.

The police station is across the way. Two men in uniform are chatting right outside the front entrance, beneath a flag snapping in the wind.

Mellie looks over at these two men. Then she goes back to staring out of the windscreen. She does not move.

Without a word, Dobbs leans across her and opens her door. The red bag is beside him.

Mellie gets out, rather hesitantly. She takes only one step, turns, and closes the car door. Her window is still open.

She is now wearing her white jacket. Dobbs knows perfectly well that she will not go to the police station. Besides, the alcohol has put her in a kind of daze: she holds onto the car with both hands. She looks at him sadly, but without hatred.

MELLIE (*softly*): What racket was Bruno Sacchi in?

DOBBS: I'm not an information centre.

The suspicion that Tony may have been involved in something illegal has been slowly invading the young woman's mind along with the whisky, and now that insidious, sultry rock tune is haunting her as well; the one Nicole was humming that first evening in her shop.

MELLIE: Please. Answer me, Mr Dobbs.

Now he is the one who seems the more irritated, who looks away in obstinate silence.

MELLIE: Things for the house, that's all Tony brings back from his trips. Or a few records for a friend.

Dobbs does not reply.

MELLIE (*imploring*): You can't hide anything in a record sleeve, can you?

More silence.

She turns away from the car and begins to walk. Not towards the police station, but in the opposite direction, towards Nicole's boutique. Mellie seems tired, a bit unsteady on her feet. Dobbs follows her with his eyes, but he doesn't move.

After stopping for a few seconds in front of the shop window, rather like the passenger from the bus two days earlier, Mellie opens the door and goes inside.

She pushes the door closed with her back.

MELLIE: Nicole!

Her friend's head pops up from behind a counter piled high with clothing. Nicole is busy taking inventory.

NICOLE: Is that you, Mellie? … Can you hang on for just a second?

Mellie is leaning back against the door, waiting. Coming towards her, Nicole is struck by her haggard expression, by the look of suffering in her eyes.

NICOLE: What's wrong?

Instead of replying, Mellie scrutinizes her friend's worried face. Standing there with an armful of sweaters, Nicole begins to lose her composure, to the point where their friendship comes to rest on the balance of this uneasy silence.

Nicole cannot bear this cold gaze any longer, and turns abruptly to some shelves, where she starts putting away – or pretending to put away – her sweaters.

MELLIE: Traitor!

Nicole whirls around at the insult, as though she's been hit. They stare at each other in silence again, until Nicole looks down.

MELLIE (*bluntly*): What have you been up to with my husband, behind my back?

Nicole no longer knows where to look. She returns to her shelves and her sweaters.

MELLIE (*shouting*): Answer me!

Nicole, whom she sees only from the back, seems to sag in defeat but then pulls herself together.

NICOLE: Oh, why not, it's better that you know … I'd rather have it all over and done with. (*Turning around.*) All right, yes, I slept with Tony, I admit it!

The sweaters she is holding slip from her hands and fall to the floor.

Mellie, whose whole world is collapsing, is unable to say a single word. Her eyes round with shock, she seems to see Nicole for the first time – or else she sees someone completely different, a woman with a superb body set off by a clinging skirt and blouse, a sensual woman, obviously attractive to men; a husband-stealer in fact, whom Tony has taken in his arms and who is trampling on Mellie's heart.

Nicole has knelt down to gather up the sweaters. She looks up at Mellie with pleading, miserable eyes.

NICOLE: You know what I was to him? … Something on the side, used once or twice, that's all. (*Standing up, her arms hanging limp.*) I swear, Mellie, it was just a brief fling, it didn't mean a thing to him, not a thing …

She approaches Mellie, who is a statue of disgust, swallowing back her tears.

NICOLE (*sincerely*): It was my fault! … I don't know what came over me …

Giving it everything she has, with a strange little moan, Mellie slaps her hard. Once, twice.

By far the stronger woman, Nicole takes the blows without protest, simply drawing her head back slightly. But when Mellie raises her hand to strike again, Nicole swiftly grabs her wrist and stops her cold.

NICOLE (*with sudden authority*): I said *twice*!

Mellie stares contemptuously at her for a few seconds more, then coolly wrenches her arm away, opens the door, and flees.

Moments later, she emerges from the small bank in Le Cap-des-Pins, further along the esplanade. As she walks towards the Dodge, parked in the sunshine, she folds up three bundles of banknotes that she carries in her hands.

It is now four o'clock, or perhaps later.

Dobbs is no longer sitting behind the wheel. She sees that he has left the red bag on the front seat, but she does not pick it up. She takes a few more steps, looking around.

He is sitting quietly on a parapet overlooking the beach. She goes to join him, walking a bit unsteadily, but with stubborn determination.

The esplanade, so crowded in the summer, is deserted. We hear only the sound of the surf. It is a late afternoon weighed down by the heavy light of autumn.

Next to Dobbs is a bottle of whisky in its brightly coloured box. His eyes, narrow against the light, contemplate the sea. He does not turn around when Mellie walks up behind him.

DOBBS (*softly*): What did you learn from your friend Nicole?

MELLIE (*in the same tone*): Nothing to interest you, Mr Dobbs.

When he does not move and keeps waiting, she shrugs wearily.

MELLIE: Tony's cheating on me with her. (*Childishly.*) I don't care.

Dobbs turns around. He no longer appears to be laughing at the world, like a cat toying with a mouse. He nods with a look of understanding that seems genuine to Mellie. That was not at all what he wanted her to find out, and he can see clearly that she does care.

She gives him the banknotes she is holding.

DOBBS: But why this money?

MELLIE: Because I'm not sure of anything anymore. ... (*Pleading.*)
Give me that photograph, Mr Dobbs.

He flips through the three bundles without enthusiasm.

She realizes he was expecting more.

MELLIE: That's all I had in the bank.

He makes a face, without answering.

MELLIE: I still have the housekeeping money at home. I'll give
you that.

He nods again, looking at her. He seems to accept her offer.

He picks up the whisky box beside him and hands it to her.

DOBBS: I bought a bottle.

He pockets the money, without taking his eyes off her. He is
wearing his insinuating half-smile again.

DOBBS: It's only right that you should pay for it, since you're the
one who's going to drink it.

She shrinks back visibly, and in her eyes we read the certainty
that he is like all blackmailers; that he will never let her go.

19

A walnut, thrown with great force, breaks in half against the glass of a French window in Mellie Mau's house.

Alone in the living room, Dobbs picks up the pieces and begins to eat the kernel as he listens to the young woman coming hesitantly downstairs.

He is sitting on a sofa.

Near him, a glass has been poured from the whisky bottle standing open on a low table. They are the first things Mellie sees when she enters the room. She has taken off her jacket. In one hand she holds the money her husband gave her the evening before.

Ignoring Dobbs, she goes straight to the full glass. She picks it up and takes a large swallow, of her own accord. She coughs, but drinks some more.

Dobbs watches her suspiciously.

DOBBS: You're starting to like it?

MELLIE: My mother says it helps you forget.

DOBBS: Forget what?

MELLIE: That men are bastards. (*Casually.*) She knows what she's talking about. When it comes to alcohol and adultery, she's unbeatable.

She throws the money she holds in her left hand at Dobbs's feet. And standing there, she swallows another mouthful of whisky.

MELLIE: Except that she's the one who was cheating on my father. (*Turning towards Dobbs.*) Well, Mr Dobbs? Pick it up!

If he is annoyed, he does not show it. He simply leans down and gathers up the banknotes. He pulls the other three bundles from his pocket and puts them all together.

DOBBS: You're paying cheaply for this murder, Love Love.

MELLIE: I'm paying to have my husband left alone, and nothing more.

The bundles of notes from the bank are secured with pins, which Dobbs removes and lets fall to the carpet.

DOBBS: Come on! Why should you be afraid for your husband?

MELLIE: Until he comes back, I have no idea. I'm buying time from you, Mr Dobbs.

He looks at the money he holds in his hand, weighing it on his fingertips. Then he throws it at Mellie's face. The banknotes scatter all over the carpet, around the startled young woman.

DOBBS: It's your turn to pick it up! (*And when she does not move.*) Pick up that money and keep it! … Do I look like the sort of man who would take a woman's housekeeping money from her?

There is so much anger in his voice that Mellie sets down her glass and obeys. While she is bending over to gather up the money, he pulls the photo of Tony from his jacket pocket, strikes a match, and sets the picture on fire.

She watches him do this. She stands up, slowly, not believing her own eyes.

MELLIE (*sincerely*): I don't understand anymore, Mr Dobbs.

He drops the burning photograph into an ashtray.

DOBBS (*cross*): I'm not a blackmailer!

MELLIE: But then, who are you?

He moves towards her with that feline grace he has. He is wearing his cat smile again. His voice becomes friendly, terribly friendly.

DOBBS: Your partner, Love Love.

She understands less and less.

DOBBS: I've been chasing Sacchi for more than a week now. I've crossed all of France and quite a bit of Germany to find him.

MELLIE: Why?

DOBBS (*coldly*): To kill him.

At first she thinks she has not heard correctly, or else she is overwhelmed by surprise. Her only reaction is to move her head ever so slightly.

Dobbs comes even closer and takes her face between his hands.

DOBBS (*in a low, tense voice*): Can you imagine how I felt when I got here, yesterday morning? Someone had already done the job for me!

She recoils instinctively and collapses into the armchair behind her.

DOBBS (*full of reproach*): Only, it was amateur work, Love Love. Me, I would have got my hands on what he was carrying in his bag.

They look into each other's eyes, he standing over her, she sitting there, trying to understand through her fear and the whisky fog.

DOBBS (*enthusiastically*): You know how much our partnership is worth? Pick a figure, Love Love.

She remains silent.

DOBBS: Sixty thousand dollars! … Sixty thousand dollars in twenties and fifties!

He snatches up two books, paperbacks, lying on a cabinet. He shows them to her, pressed tightly together in his hands.

DOBBS: Makes a stack of money this thick!

He tosses the books back onto the cabinet.

MELLIE: The police didn't find that money with the body?

DOBBS (*impatiently*): No! And it wasn't in his bag, either! And I know for sure that you haven't got it!

MELLIE (*delighted*): Well, so?

DOBBS: So, you are going to tell me exactly how you killed him! … And I'll take care of the rest!

She tries to draw herself up, but he simply shoves her back into the armchair.

And now, from under his jacket, behind his back, he draws out a big Luger with a steely blue barrel. He weighs the gun in his hand, in front of her. Mellie shrinks back in fright, swallowing hard.

MELLIE: I've never killed anyone!

For a moment, she thinks he is going to hit her with his weapon. He draws back his arm roughly as though to do so, but it is only to scare her. He touches his wristwatch with the pistol barrel.

DOBBS: I've wasted a lot of time with you!

He stops abruptly, looking down at his watch. He has an idea.

DOBBS: It's almost six. The clock in the hall is about to strike, Love Love.

He moves just a little further off. He flips off the safety catch on the Luger and coldly aims the gun at Mellie's head.

DOBBS: I'll give you until the last stroke of six to tell me you killed him. Otherwise … (*He cocks the automatic.*) I'll kill you!

Slumped in her chair, appalled, Mellie cannot take her eyes off the gun pointed at her. She is paralysed. Hardly able to breathe. In the lengthening silence, we can hear her gasping for breath.

MELLIE (*very softly*): I swear I'm telling you the truth!

DOBBS (*just as softly*): So am I.

He remains quite still.

MELLIE (*gasping*): I don't believe you.

DOBBS: Same here.

He doesn't move a millimetre.

The most frightening thing of all is that the tension is getting to him, too: we can hear his breathing, and he seems fascinated by the suspense, by the expression of terror on Mellie's face.

All of a sudden, the clock strikes. First the carillon that precedes the chimes, and then the chimes themselves, inexorably counting out the hour.

Mellie tries to sink deeper into her armchair. Dobbs has become unrecognizable: he wants her to speak, he wills it.

At the third stroke of the clock, Mellie shakes her head desperately and whimpers. At the fifth, she squeezes her eyes closed but immediately opens them again in frantic bewilderment. She sees Dobbs's finger tightening on the trigger. The clock strikes six. He fires.

Braced in her chair, clutching the armrests with both hands, her head thrown back as though she were already dead, Mellie hears a click – and nothing more.

When she opens her eyes, Dobbs is still in front of her, but his arm is hanging by his side, the Luger pointed at the floor. He looks weary.

DOBBS (*with a sigh*): Bravo.

He moves away, without taking his eyes off Mellie, pulling a small, flat, black object from one of his pockets.

DOBBS: You must have seen that it wasn't loaded.

He shoves the object – a loading-clip – into the empty grip of the Luger and tucks the gun back under his jacket. He is himself again. He waits for her reply, but Mellie, sprawled in her chair, is still trying to catch her breath and recover her wits.

DOBBS: You've certainly earned a drink, Love Love.

He goes towards the low table. He pours her a brimming glass of whisky. His back is turned when the young woman calls out to him.

MELLIE: On the rocks!

Dobbs freezes, bottle in hand. And then, he nods, with a faint smile. She really has got a nerve.

20

With a tearing sound, Mellie pulls on the lever of the ice tray to dislodge the cubes. She drops two of them into her glass. Mellie and Dobbs are in the kitchen. Dobbs is leaning against the fridge.

MELLIE: How did you wind up at Le Cap-des-Pins?

DOBBS: I talked to the bus driver.

Mellie slowly rubs an ice cube across her forehead, then along her cheeks.

MELLIE: And why did you come to the wedding?

DOBBS: Your friend Nicole told me you'd be there.

MELLIE (*glowering*): She's not my friend. She's a tuba.

She puts the ice tray down by the sink.

DOBBS: A what?

MELLIE: Whenever I need to use a swearword, I say 'tuba'. (*Drying her hands.*) Of all the ones I know, you're the one who makes the most noise.

He just smiles.

There is a strange, vague understanding between the two of them now. They both know, after the crisis of the chimes at six o'clock, that they are fighting a duel over Mellie's confession; and that the winner will be the one who holds out the longest.

MELLIE: Maybe Sacchi didn't have that money anymore by the time he came to Le Cap-des-Pins?

Dobbs thrusts two fingers into the breast pocket of his jacket and pulls out a green note, which he unfolds in front of her: twenty dollars.

DOBBS: He paid for the bus ride with this.

MELLIE: That doesn't prove anything.

DOBBS: Bring your glass, and I will prove something to you.

She obeys. But while he heads towards the living room, she pours half her whisky into the sink. She follows him with the slow steps of a sleepwalker.

Dobbs is standing in front of the chest beneath the gun rack.

A few feet away from him, Mellie leans back against the wall, glass in hand.

DOBBS: In this drawer, there is a box with two cartridges missing.

MELLIE (*drunk, but calm*): I'd be surprised.

DOBBS: I searched the house while you were at the airport. (*Forcefully.*) There are two cartridges missing!

MELLIE: I'd be surprised.

Dobbs looks at her, a bit shaken by her composure. He opens the drawer without taking his eyes off her. And then he pulls out a cellophane-wrapped box, identical to the one she opened to shoot the passenger from the bus. This box, however, is brand new.

Dobbs tears off the wrapper, checks to see that no cartridges are missing, and tosses the box onto the chest.

DOBBS: You bought a fresh one this morning.

Mellie looks away, unruffled.

DOBBS: Drink.

She obeys. One swallow. Meanwhile, Dobbs gets down from the rack the double-barrelled shotgun she used.

Fear returns to Mellie's eyes.

DOBBS: And this? … Anyone can smell that this gun has recently been fired. An expert will tell you it was the day before yesterday.

She stares at the weapon. Now it is her turn to look disconcerted, but she does not reply.

DOBBS: Well, go on, say it's not true!

MELLIE (*quite unexpectedly*): It's true.

Her answer leaves him nonplussed. He looks at the gun, then back at the young woman, who stands ramrod straight, holding her glass.

DOBBS: You admit it?

MELLIE: The day before yesterday … I shot at some rats in the basement.

She points to the basement door.

DOBBS (*dumbfounded*): Rats?

Mellie nods uneasily and takes a sip of whisky.

Dobbs drops the gun onto the chest and marches confidently towards the basement.

DOBBS: Come along, Love Love.

He opens the door and flicks on the light. He turns around to make sure she is following him.

She is. He goes down the stairs. With a grim look on her face, Mellie pauses by the chest and sets down her glass. She picks up the gun with one hand and plucks two cartridges from the open box. She moves on towards the door, walking slowly, loading the gun. She stops at the head of the stairs.

Below, in the light of the bare bulb, everything is the same as it was that morning. The dinghy still lies upside down on the floor.

Dobbs turns on another light near the boiler, illuminating the wall that separates the basement from the garage. Now the bullet holes in the concrete wall can be clearly seen, at shoulder height.

DOBBS (*smiling*): Rats? That high?

Framed in the doorway, holding the gun behind her back, Mellie gestures with her free hand, vaguely tracing a leap in the air.

MELLIE: They were jumping!

This is too silly. Still smiling, Dobbs shakes his head. He is standing between the basement and the garage, a friendly wild animal. Of course he has noticed that Mellie is holding the shotgun, but it does not seem to worry him.

DOBBS: Listen, Love Love. This would be proof for even the dumbest cop. But I'm not a cop. I'm a future millionaire. Tell me the truth.

Mellie's only reply is to point the shotgun straight at him.

DOBBS: What are you doing?

MELLIE (*drunkenly*): I'm aiming at a future millionaire! (*Vengefully.*) And I'm not going to wait for the clock to strike!

Dobbs hits the floor in a rolling dive as Mellie fires. The shot strikes the wall.

They are both silent after the discharge. Mellie is still wrought up. She swings the gun around quickly at Dobbs, to keep him at a distance. Dobbs is incensed.

He has got to his feet and begun to climb the steps, his face contorted with rage.

MELLIE (*shouting*): Don't move!

She gets him in her sights again, and he stops short on the stairs. She is breathing hard. She is drunk, not simply from the whisky but from too many things that have shattered her nerves. She is quite capable of pulling the second trigger and actually killing him this time.

MELLIE (*in a strained voice*): Well? Go for your gun, Mr Dobbs!

He does not move a muscle.

MELLIE: I didn't kill Sacchi!

She swings the gun barrels around again, aims at the concrete wall pockmarked by lead shot, and fires. Chips of concrete spin through the air. Dobbs does not even flinch at this new explosion.

MELLIE (*lowering her weapon*): So, where's your proof now?

Dobbs is suddenly on the move again, taut with icy fury. His eyes are terrifying.

And she is terrified. She steps back, cold sober, with the look of a child who has broken a porcelain vase and knows she will pay dearly for it.

She flees.

First she runs to the front door, but it is jammed, and she cannot get it open, and Dobbs is already in the living room.

Then she races to the stairs, clambering up them two at a time, grimacing with fear. She trips and drops the gun. She hears Dobbs's footsteps behind her: he is not bothering to hurry, certain that she cannot escape him.

Too bad about the gun. She rushes into her bedroom.

She closes and locks the door. She dashes straight to the bathroom, through which Dobbs could get in, and she bolts the door leading to Tony's bedroom.

Looking hunted, she returns to her room.

She had not realized this, but in the time she and Dobbs have been in the basement, daylight has ebbed away, and evening has arrived. Now only the vivid glow of sunset pours through the windows. Everything in the room has turned red and grey.

And Mellie's bedroom door flies open with a crash, at a single kick from Dobbs, who couldn't care less about locks.

The door has been violently pushed open by a man in a vest. And it is not the same door anymore: this one belongs to a modest apartment, the kind you enter through the kitchen. The man moves aside, with the look of someone who has done what was asked of him, and it is Juliette who steps through the front door, bewildered, with a trembling Mellie, nine years old, close on her heels. Mother and daughter make straight for the bedroom, which we have seen before, where everything is in a shambles. Drawers have been pulled out of the chests and tables; mattress stuffing is scattered all over the floor. They are still wearing their coats. Mellie gazes through her tears at this dismal sight, while Juliette cries out, but we cannot hear a thing. There is a shiny ten-franc piece on the floor, a pretty coin that little Mellie picks up with real fingernails and will never forget for the rest of her life.

Dobbs has entered the room with a stony face and a terrible

look in his eyes. He pushes the broken door closed with his back.

Mellie is cowering against a wall.

Dobbs turns on the light. The room, their expressions – everything changes abruptly.

Only a few feet separate them, and she is afraid. He had told her he would spank her, and that is just what she is afraid of; but we can see that she is more ashamed than afraid.

Yet his mind is on something quite different from spanking her or wasting time.

DOBBS: Lift that up!

He points to her blouse. Mellie looks at him with panic in her eyes. He does not move, stares at her coldly. Slowly, she obeys. She pulls the blouse free of her skirt and lifts it up. On her bare skin, over her stomach, a bruise is clearly visible: blue or mauve, ugly, vile.

DOBBS (*in a different voice*): Who hit you?

She lets her blouse fall back down. She is overwhelmed by the drink and by her humiliation, but once more, the stubborn girl inside her finds an answer.

MELLIE: It was Tony, last night.

DOBBS (*trying to control his temper*): Tony? … Why?

MELLIE: He saw me dancing with you.

Dobbs no longer believes a word she says, but at that, he shakes his head, as if dazed. And then he grabs her by her shoulders and lifts her as though she were a feather, bringing her face right up to his. He is beside himself, but how can he insult her, what can he say?

DOBBS: Tuba!

And he throws her roughly back on the bed.

She simply bounces back up again. Suddenly on her feet, she faces him from the other side of the bed. She tries to hit him when he leans towards her. She misses.

MELLIE (*like a child*): Tony's coming home tonight! He'll punch your face in! He knows how to fight!

DOBBS (*curtly*): So do I!

We can tell he has no desire, for the moment, to argue anymore. He straightens up.

DOBBS (*wearily*): Tony won't be back until the day after tomorrow. You'll never hold out that long, Love Love.

She dashes into the bathroom but cannot wrench the other door open. She has always had problems with doors. Dobbs goes quietly over and unbolts the door for her.

He does not look at her, but goes back out into the hall.

Mellie listens to him going downstairs.

A moment later, in the bathroom with both doors closed, she catches sight of her face in the mirror over the sink.

The passenger from the bus is struggling with her, Tuesday evening, and with both hands she tears the stocking concealing his face, and he drives his fist into her stomach. There is no cry, nothing but the sound of Mellie's breathing.

She is in front of the mirror, looking at herself.

The clock, downstairs, begins to strike. One chime, two, three.

Mellie stares into her own eyes. Four, five, six. She is ashamed of what she has just done, ashamed of her memories, and now she cannot look herself in the face anymore.

Seven, eight. The clock continues striking, relentlessly.

21

Nine, ten, eleven chimes.

How many hours have passed, no one will ever know.

Kneeling on the rug in the living room, Mellie is inside a kind of pen. Dobbs has drawn armchairs and sofas up around her so that she cannot escape. She is completely surrounded. She is still wearing her white blouse and skirt.

The duel, it seems, has continued. Dobbs has been doing well. He is perched on the back of an armchair in his shirt sleeves, with his tie undone, eating a sandwich and drinking some milk, listening to Mellie with the air of a wild animal at rest, observing her through half-closed eyes.

Beneath a single lighted lamp, Mellie is talking. And has been for a long time. Drunkenly, with infinite lassitude.

MELLIE: … The day my father left, I found a coin on the floor … The door was locked. So we went to get a neighbour and he broke it down … In the bedroom, the mess was unbelievable …

On a coffee table she spreads out the money she tried to give Dobbs, lining up the notes like playing cards arranged for a game of patience. She looks up at him.

MELLIE: My father had even used the mattress cover to wrap his things up in! … That's right, the ticking! … It's true, Mr Dobbs.

DOBBS: Why did he leave?

MELLIE (*after a pause*): Because I saw my mother in bed with another man! … Oh, after all, what do I care. (*Growing suddenly cross.*) My father asked me questions, and more questions, and more questions, and finally I couldn't take it anymore, and I told him everything! … So, that's it … And he left.

Dobbs notices that Mellie's glass, which she is pressing against her forehead, now holds nothing but a few ice cubes. He comes over to pour her another stiff whisky and then sits down on the arm of a sofa.

MELLIE (*sadly*): It's my fault. Right.

She sips at her glass. Dobbs leans down so that he can be almost at her level when he speaks to her.

DOBBS: I understand, Love Love: you confessed once and it worked out badly for you. So now you can't ever admit anything again.

Mellie turns aside and gives a disparaging little laugh.

MELLIE: You and your psychology! (*Looking at him intently.*) If I'd killed that man, I'd have gone straight to the police!

DOBBS (*bluntly*): No! Not after what he did to you! Women who've been through that don't go to the police.

MELLIE: More psychology?

DOBBS: No, just statistics. (*Standing up.*) I'm unbeatable at statistics.

Mellie opens her eyes wide, staring at him. And she tries to get to her feet, furious, intending to throw her drink in his face. He does not move. She has just managed to stand up when a car horn is heard outside.

Dobbs turns off the light instantly. He goes over to the French windows to look out into the garden.

MELLIE: Who's coming to rescue me, Mr Dobbs?

DOBBS: Don't move.

It is Nicole. Behind the glass door, Dobbs watches her get out of her car – a small Austin – and walk towards the house in the pale moonlight. The gravel crunches beneath her feet.

She rings the bell. Then she knocks on the front door.

NICOLE (*outside*): Mellie! … Please, open up!

Silence.

Finding the door unlocked, she enters the house. The kitchen is now the only room with a light on.

NICOLE (*softly*): Mellie, I know you're here! ... You have to listen to me! ... Mellie?

She walks slowly towards the living room. Then Mellie does something extraordinary. She throws her arms around Harry Dobbs and kisses him on the lips. Taken aback at first, Dobbs realizes that Mellie wants to shock Nicole, and he plays along with her game.

The lights go on. Nicole stands in the doorway openmouthed at the sight of two lovers kissing passionately, completely unaffected by her presence.

NICOLE (*in a toneless voice*): Sorry ... I thought you were alone.

The two lovers pull a few centimetres apart to look at her.

DOBBS (*grinning*): Mellie's busy this evening.

Nicole whirls around in dismay and rushes out without a word. We can hear her running across the gravel drive. Then her car engine starts up.

Mellie flops down onto the rug and looks around her in discouragement.

MELLIE: My life is like this house. Only two days ago, everything was perfectly in order. Now people are kicking in doors, blasting away in the cellar with guns, polishing off bottles of Scotch, kissing ... (*She looks up.*) ... anyone at all ... Do you know why I kissed you, Mr Dobbs?

DOBBS (*smiling at this easy question*): Because you're in love with me.

She shrugs. But she seems in better spirits too, as he does. He takes some walnuts out of his pocket. Three of them. He is standing next to her. He drops them into her skirt.

She picks them up, tired, and drunk, and what the hell. She gets bravely to her feet, facing the French windows. Holding herself very straight, trying not to stand there swaying, she throws a walnut at the glass. A pane breaks and the pieces shiver to the floor. She gestures in resignation.

Dobbs nods, heaves a little sigh.

DOBBS: You're going to say that you kissed me to get back at Nicole. It's true, partly. But there's something else.

Exhausted, she has half lain down on a sofa, her face resting among the scattered banknotes.

DOBBS: The last thing you want is for someone else to start poking around in our business. And find out anything …

She does not answer. He goes over to her.

DOBBS (*gently*): Love Love?

She has fallen asleep, simply fallen asleep, poleaxed by the strain and the alcohol. Her face seems sad and lost.

Her white blouse has ridden up a little above the bruise on her stomach. Dobbs pulls it back down.

He slips on his jacket to leave.

In the entrance hall, he takes one of Mellie's coats down from its peg, a white coat, and he returns to cover her with it.

He does this with surprising care and gentleness. Then he looks at her, expressionless, for some time. He notices that she is still holding two walnuts in her right hand. He removes them from her grasp and puts them in a pocket of her coat, so that she will find them when she awakens.

As he goes towards the door, he stumbles over a red bag sitting on the rug. It is the bag belonging to the passenger from the bus. Wearily, and with a strange distaste, Dobbs kicks the bag out of his way.

And then he looks back at Mellie lying asleep. He is on his own, a lone wild animal, and he turns out the lights on a battlefield where victory has eluded him once again.

Friday, 10 a.m.

22

Covered with her coat, Mellie is sleeping on the sofa. She must be having a bad dream, or else the sunlight flooding in through the windows is disturbing her, because her hands clutch at the white woollen material, and she whimpers.

She opens her eyes. And sees her mother sitting near her, watching her sleep.

Mellie throws off the coat and begins to get up. Too quickly. There is a violent pounding in her skull, so awful that she puts her head in her hands. A hangover that is no less colossal for all that it is the first one she's ever had.

Juliette observes her in silence, with compassion and a twinkling of irony.

Mellie manages to sit up. Juliette collects the money strewn everywhere and stacks the notes into a bundle that she gives to Mellie.

Without saying anything, without paying any further attention to her boozer of a daughter, Juliette gets a duster and begins cleaning up a house that appears to have been hit by a hurricane.

Later, sitting outside on the terrace in her monogrammed bathrobe, Mellie is drinking a large cup of coffee.

It is a glorious morning.

The young woman has had a bath; her hair is still damp. She seems to have recovered somewhat, but the sunshine hurts her eyes.

Sounds are particularly distressing. They are quite muffled, and yet every one is painful. Even the footsteps of her mother, who emerges from the house and comes over to her.

JULIETTE: My cars that needed fixing, did you drop them off?

Mellie looks up from her coffee cup and blinks at her mother without understanding.

MELLIE: Your what?

JULIETTE (*waving her hand*): Vroom! Vroom! … My little cars!

Mellie winces guiltily.

MELLIE: No. I forgot all about them.

JULIETTE: Where are they?

MELLIE (*after a moment's thought*): In my car.

Juliette goes over to the station-wagon parked in the drive, not far from the front steps.

MELLIE (*trying to make amends*): I'll take them in today!

JULIETTE: Certainly not. I'll do it. That way, it will get done.

Mellie finishes her coffee.

Juliette opens the boot of the Dodge and pulls the cardboard box sitting behind the back seat towards her. She opens the box and looks inside.

JULIETTE: Is this yours?

Mellie looks up. Her mother shows her a red bag she has just lifted out of the big box. A red bag absolutely identical to the one Mellie picked up at the left-luggage room in the station. You would think it was the same bag.

JULIETTE: Are you starting a collection?

She brings it over to an amazed Mellie and without another word goes off to her own car – a white Renault – with her box under her arm.

While Juliette starts her car, Mellie unzips the bag with a kind of dread. One glance shows her that there is money inside – green notes – spilling out of a page of newspaper wrapped around them. Dollars, several thick bundles of dollars.

She watches her mother drive away, then rises and goes into the house with the bag.

The armchairs have been put back where they belong. Clearly visible, sitting on one of them, is the red bag picked up at the station.

Mellie goes over and lifts it up. She holds a red bag in each hand.

She looks at each one in turn, puzzled, trying to understand. Then the light dawns and her face is convulsed with pure rage, rage at having been fooled, at having fallen into a trap. Dobbs has tricked her. And now she can think of nothing else.

23

At the wheel of the Dodge, Mellie pulls up in a silent and deserted garden in front of a large white building in turn-of-the-century style: the Palm Hotel. All the windows are shuttered, except for one on the second floor.

Before getting out of her car, Mellie takes off her dark glasses and looks at that window.

In an equally silent and deserted corridor, she knocks on the door of room number eighteen.

She is wearing her white coat, her high-heeled shoes, and is carrying one of the two red bags. Only one.

Since no one answers from inside the room, and the key is in the lock, she opens the door.

She knows immediately that this is indeed Harry Dobbs's room: she steps on a nutshell lying on the carpet. And there is a large bag of walnuts sitting open on a table cluttered with files and a typewriter. An ashtray overflows with empty nutshells.

She closes the door behind her.

She crosses the room and goes first of all to the adjoining bathroom to check that no one is there.

She sees men's toiletries, a red towelling dressing gown.

The room's curtains are red as well.

Mellie opens a large wardrobe. Only two hangers are in use, but what is on them stuns her: an army trenchcoat and the brown uniform of an American officer. The gold braid and decorations on the jacket indicate – although Mellie does not yet realize this – the rank of colonel.

Confused, she goes over to the typewriter, which sits on a table between two windows.

She looks at the sheet of paper rolled into the typewriter. It bears the heading of the American embassy in Bonn.

As she straightens up to examine the room again, she fails to notice that behind her, framed in one of the windows, Dobbs's red Ford Mustang is coming up the hotel drive.

She goes over to a suitcase lying flat on a luggage stand. She opens it. Clean clothes, military and civilian. The big Luger she saw the previous day. A frame with a photograph of a cute little boy, smiling, quite tanned.

There is an identification tag chained to the suitcase handle. Mellie reads it.

COLONEL HARRY C. DOBBS

U.S. ARMY

She hears rapid footsteps out in the hall. With no idea where to hide, she dashes into the bathroom.

Dobbs opens the door almost at once. And the first thing he sees is the red bag, on the bed.

He comes in, closes the door behind him. He glances at the open bathroom as he takes off his jacket. Then he removes his shirt. Stripped to the waist, he takes a second to unzip the red bag, just to make sure it is the one picked up at the station.

And then, abruptly, he enters the bathroom, reaches behind the door and grabs Mellie, dragging her roughly out by one arm.

Mellie has managed not to cry out. She is extremely uneasy to be finding herself like this in the bedroom of a man who is half undressed. This was Dobbs's intention.

DOBBS (*harshly*): I let women in my room for only one reason! And I choose them before I do so!

Mellie recoils, even more upset. He seems made of muscles, he really is a brute. Still, she stands up to him.

MELLIE: Well, you came and snooped all over my house! ... Yesterday morning you stole a photograph of my husband and put it inside this bag! Your bag! And it was you who left it in the left-luggage at the station! ... You invented that whole story! Tony never had anything to do with all this!

DOBBS: Right. But if you know that, it means you've found the other red bag, the real one.

The young woman does not bat an eyelid.

MELLIE: No ... I worked it out. And now I know who you are, Colonel Dobbs! ... A policeman!

Unfazed, Dobbs puts his shirt back on.

DOBBS: Not a policeman. Let's say I'm conducting a parallel investigation.

MELLIE: Why?

DOBBS: In the army, you don't ask why.

He walks around to the other side of the table.

DOBBS: I have to find out the truth, send in a report, and that's all.

He types with one finger, very quickly, on the typewriter keyboard. He turns the machine around so that Mellie can read: MURDER.

He comes back towards her.

DOBBS: And the truth is what you're going to tell me, here. I'm even going to help you. I'm going to say it for you.

Mellie backs away a bit, at his approach, but listens to him carefully.

DOBBS: Tuesday evening, a stranger surprised you alone, in your home ... He had a stocking over his face ... You tried to defend yourself, and then he hit you!

Mellie stares at him in horror. She senses that he wants to throw her into the same state of panic she felt on Tuesday night.

DOBBS: Like this!

He only pretends to throw a punch, but she shields her stomach instinctively with her hands.

DOBBS (*satisfied*): You see?

Then he picks her up, cradling her in his arms as though she weighed next to nothing. She is speechless with surprise and fright.

DOBBS: Now I'll tell you what he did to you next!

And he throws her onto the bed.

He comes after her with a great leap, and stands towering over her. She is dizzy and disoriented.

Naked, suffocating, she falls back onto the bed in her own room, as her hands are tied behind her. And it is the passenger from the bus who is on top of her, turning her over, forcing her to look at him, as though she were a doll without hands or arms.

She makes a sound that is more of a moan than a scream, and she opens her eyes in the hotel room, clutching her temples. Dobbs, bestriding her on his knees, bends down over her face. He speaks faster, louder; he senses that he has her now.

DOBBS: He didn't leave the house when he had finished! He always hung around afterwards! I know this guy by heart – I can read files! You found him in the cellar and you killed him!

She shakes her head frantically, but she cannot utter a word. She is stretched out on the bed, her clothing in disarray, with a vicious headache hammering her skull. Dobbs is like a boxer who has seized an opening and wants to wind things up with a knock-out.

DOBBS: And I've got proof! First you called the police, that evening, but you hung up without saying anything! That I found out from the operator!

She keeps her eyes closed. He tallies the evidence on his fingers as he talks.

DOBBS: To get rid of the body, you went out late at night. You bumped into a police road block. That I found out from the police station!

She does not even react anymore. He has only to finish her off.

DOBBS (*finishing her off*): And at the police road block, you said you were going to get your husband at the airport! It wasn't true! That I found out from your mother!

All of a sudden, with her face pressed against the bed, she opens one eye. A strange and startling eye. Before she replies, he already knows just from the look in this eye that he has said one word too many, that she has just caught hold of something to break her fall.

She speaks with Juliette's cutting tone, uses Juliette's words.

MELLIE: Certainly not. My mother never says a thing.

She raises herself up a little. Watchful and defiant, she looks at him. He has nothing more to say and can tell that once again, she is getting away from him.

MELLIE: I'm going to ask you a question, Mr Dobbs. If you know everything, if you have all your proof, why have you put on this act with me?

He does not answer. He moves away. She sits up on the bed, without taking her eyes off him, thinking things over.

MELLIE: You've tried everything to make me confess. Which means you must be missing some crucial element. Which one, Mr Dobbs?

He still does not answer. In his eyes we can see fatigue, disappointment, but something else as well: that look of friendly understanding – as though the truest part of himself admires how Mellie defends herself so courageously. He points his finger at her.

DOBBS (*wearily*): Bravo.

She stands up and heads for the door. He does not try to stop her. He buttons up his white shirt. When she struggles impatiently with the doorknob, he just walks over and flips up the latch.

MELLIE (*softly*): I didn't kill him, Mr Dobbs.

He does not reply, and allows her to leave. He has one more card to play – a good one. Unperturbed, he follows her into the empty corridor.

DOBBS: You'll confess anyway, Love Love. You're not the type to let an innocent woman be accused in your place.

She stops short, but refuses to turn around.

DOBBS: They've arrested Sacchi's mistress.

At that Mellie does turn around, with a look of misery on her face.

MELLIE: It's not true!

DOBBS: At this very moment they're down on the beach where they found the body. Go and see for yourself …

It takes Mellie a moment to react.

MELLIE (*uneasily*): If she's innocent, she has nothing to fear.

DOBBS: What a joke. Even his friends are after her hide. You know why? (*Confidently.*) As far as they're concerned, she's the one who kept the sixty thousand dollars!

Mellie shakes her head, still refusing to believe it. Dobbs shrugs and turns away.

MELLIE: What beach?

That smile. Those narrowed eyes.

DOBBS: You think the body drifted?

MELLIE: I don't think anything! I don't know anything!

She starts down the stairs. Dobbs leans over the bannisters, smiling.

DOBBS: A place called La Pelouque!

Mellie blinks, nothing more. She continues down the stairs, slowly, concealing her eagerness to get to that beach.

24

L a Pelouque.
In the noonday sun, the face of the woman who has been arrested: a face without expression, beautiful and grave. The woman is about thirty, blonde, wearing clothes that are fashionable but rather creased; and she has the defeated look of someone who has not slept, who has been pushed around and questioned relentlessly.

She stands motionless before a gaping hole dug in the sand. Around her are plainclothes policemen, officers in uniform, the deputy public prosecutor – the machinery of the law in action.

The beach is vast and empty, except for two children playing, a boy and a girl, who are jumping back and forth over the hole. Inspector Toussaint shoos them away. The only sounds are the rushing of the wind and the rustle of the waves dying away on the shore.

Mellie is at the wheel of her car, which is parked near those of the police. She watches the group from a distance, through her windscreen, torn between the need to run over to the police to rescue this woman she does not know and the physical fear of being caught herself, hauled off to prison, far from Tony, far from everything.

She gets out of the Dodge.

She sees that the woman, accompanied by two policemen, has started walking back to the cars. Mellie watches her approach: head high, looking solemn but composed.

And then, she sees the man who seems to be in charge – the deputy public prosecutor – say something to Toussaint, who hurries on ahead to his own car.

Mellie runs over to him.

She reaches him just as he has found the file he has been sent for and is closing his car door.

MELLIE (*out of breath*): Toussaint!

TOUSSAINT (*stopping*): Yes?

MELLIE: I … I've got something to tell you.

TOUSSAINT (*apologetically*): Excuse me, Mellie, but this is hardly the moment.

MELLIE (*pleading*): Toussaint! … Who is that woman?

TOUSSAINT: Sacchi's mistress. She used to rent a house, up there. Her name is Madeleine Legauff.

MELLIE (*detaining him*): She doesn't live here anymore?

TOUSSAINT (*in a hurry, but trying to be nice*): No. They brought her here from Paris, yesterday evening. She's a hostess in a restaurant at the Eiffel Tower.

MELLIE: Then why did they arrest her?

TOUSSAINT: Well, she was here when the murder was committed.

He moves off, his file tucked under his arm, but looks back after a few moments with a grin of astonishment.

TOUSSAINT: Hey, Mellie, this story really interests you!

Mellie returns sadly to the Dodge. The accused woman walks by, flanked by her police escorts, as Mellie settles herself behind the wheel.

Their eyes meet.

The unfortunate suspect is helped into the back seat of the police car parked next to the Dodge, and so the two women are briefly quite close to one another.

They stare at each other, framed through the two car windows. Madeleine Legauff is doubtless surprised by the teary-eyed, almost supplicating look on the face of this unknown woman, but the very pride with which she bears up under it takes on a different meaning for Mellie: this woman is judging her, she is a living reproach.

The police car drives away.

Overcome by emotion, Mellie drops her head into her hands and leans against the steering wheel.

Almost immediately, sensing a nearby presence, she looks up: the little girl who was playing on the beach a few minutes earlier is standing quite still next to the car, watching her silently.

MELLIE (*imploringly*): Go away … Don't look at me … You hear me, go away!

The child turns and runs off.

In the distance, on the rocks that overlook the beach, sitting alone, his forearms crossed over one raised knee, Harry Dobbs sees everything. His face is impassive. He looks like a cat, waiting.

25

The sixty thousand dollars form two fat bundles on top of a bureau in Mellie's bedroom.

Wearing white gloves, the young woman shoves the money into a large manila envelope.

Her movements are hurried, but slightly mechanical, slowed down by headache and fatigue.

She opens a cupboard and stands on tiptoe to reach up for a hatbox on the top shelf. The box falls, spilling its contents across the rug. Mellie bends over to gather everything up. Among the scattered objects she discovers the ten-franc piece she once found on the floor in the wreckage of a ruined bedroom.

She holds the coin in her hand for a moment, but does not want to linger over memories. Quickly, she piles everything into the hatbox, along with the empty bag belonging to the passenger from the bus.

As she puts the box back at the top of the closet, she feels dizzy, and has to cling to the shelf.

To the sound of a pounding heartbeat, Mellie, in a white coat, steps out of a taxi and turns around to look up: she is beneath the enormous metal legs of the Eiffel Tower.

Pulling herself together, the young woman goes to her bed, places the brown envelope inside a small leather travel bag, and closes the bag. She puts on her coat to leave.

She freezes when she hears a sound downstairs that is beginning to be familiar: the sharp crack of something striking a pane of glass and splitting in two. She goes over to a window: Dobbs's Ford

Mustang is parked outside, behind the Dodge.

Now that the cat has arrived, Mellie becomes as quiet as a mouse. Carrying her travel bag, she goes slowly and carefully down the stairs, bypasses the living room, and leaves the house through the kitchen.

Walking on the grass by the edge of the driveway, she goes over to the red Mustang. She opens the door gently, removes the key from the ignition, and throws it far away.

Without closing the door, she walks over to her own car. She tosses the leather bag onto the floor mat next to her feet as she gets in behind the wheel.

At the sound of her engine starting up, Dobbs shoots out of the house like a jack-in-the-box. He runs full tilt across the garden to cut her off.

She must drive in a sweeping arc to reach the front gate. She drives quickly, but Dobbs gets there before she does. She must slam on the brakes to keep from running him over.

He stands squarely in front of the Dodge, steady on his feet, and clearly has no intention of letting her pass.

Shifting sharply into reverse, Mellie lurches the car back a few yards, shifts again, and drives forward, heading straight for Dobbs. She is no longer in a normal state. She is at the end of her tether, the end of her anguish, the end of everything.

MELLIE (*shouting*): Get out of the way!

Dobbs has just enough time to leap aside as the Dodge hurtles past. Mellie swings out of the gate and drives off at top speed. Dobbs goes over to his Mustang, sees that the key is no longer in the ignition. He calms down, and slams the car door shut. He has a new idea.

26

Marseille–Marignane.
Mellie's midnight-blue station-wagon is in a corner of the airport car park.

The red Ford Mustang is sitting beside the Dodge, with its hood up. Dobbs is bending over the engine, removing the jumper wire he attached to the ignition coil to start the car.

DOBBS (*straightening up*): I lost the key.

He is speaking, in English, to two stern-looking men in suits and ties standing nearby. The older man has a well-trimmed beard; the other could pass for an important bank executive or lawyer or what he probably is, an officer of the military police.

THE FIRST MAN: She took a plane to Paris.

DOBBS (*closing the hood*): Did you inform the embassy?

THE FIRST MAN (*curtly*): They'll try to detain her at Orly. But I don't wish to be involved in this … I do not approve of your methods, Colonel Dobbs.

DOBBS (*placidly*): That's your problem.

THE FIRST MAN (*more sharply*): The body from Le Cap-des-Pins is not the man you're looking for. He was killed over a year ago! This woman has nothing to do with that!

Dobbs does not back down. His eyes become two crafty little slits again.

DOBBS: If she's confusing the two of them, it's because the man I'm looking for is dead, too.

THE FIRST MAN: You assume. And if you're wrong?

DOBBS (*hands on hips*): I'm not wrong.

THE FIRST MAN (*angrily*): You deceived her! Thanks to you, she's going to stick her nose into something really nasty.

He emphasizes this last word: *nasty*.

THE FIRST MAN: How are you going to get her out of this mess?

DOBBS (*with a smile*): That's *my* problem.

He looks at his watch.

DOBBS: Has she got much of a lead on me?

The second man checks his watch, too.

THE SECOND MAN: She should be landing just about now.

Dobbs does not seem at all worried. He simply holds out his hand expectantly. The second man pulls an aeroplane ticket from his jacket and gives it to Dobbs.

Without saying goodbye, without even looking at the two other men, the American walks away, with his light, catlike step, towards the airport terminal.

In the sky, a jet soars overhead, powerful, majestic.

27

Orly.
    Wearing dark glasses and carrying her travel bag, Mellie Mau goes up a flight of stairs to the arrivals hall along with other passengers who have just landed at the airport.

Chimes are heard. A woman's silken voice comes over the loudspeakers.

'Would Madame Mélancolie Mau, arriving from Marseille–Marignane, please go to the information desk ...'

Mellie has halted in surprise for only a second. The announcement is repeated over the loudspeakers, but Mellie quickens her pace, glancing furtively about her, eager to escape from the airport.

Later, Mellie steps out of a taxi, hands the fare to the driver. When she turns around and looks up, she is standing – for real, this time – beneath the enormous metal legs of the Eiffel Tower.

Still later, another taxi lets her off on the Champs-Élysées.

She walks over to a yellow letter-box and drops in the stamped and addressed brown envelope containing the sixty thousand dollars.

A moment later, she places a call from a public phone booth. God only knows what she is saying, but she is insistent, animated.

It is at about the same moment, no doubt, that Harry Dobbs, wearing a black tie with his tweed jacket, pushes through the revolving door of the restaurant on the second level of the Eiffel Tower, following the same path that Mellie must have taken.

Even later still, Mellie rings a doorbell somewhere in the Paris night.

A man studies her through the spy hole, then waves her inside.

We are in a richly and somewhat gaudily furnished private town house. Down a white hallway decorated with wall hangings and large vases comes a very tall, very blonde hostess wearing an extremely low-cut evening gown.

MELLIE (*timidly*): I have an appointment with Tania Legauff.

THE HOSTESS (*holding out her hand*): I know. Would you please hand me your coat and bag.

MELLIE: No, no, thank you, I'll keep them with me.

The hostess's commanding smile disappears. She continues to hold out her hand.

THE HOSTESS (*rather curtly*): That was not a question.

Mellie obeys, gives the woman her travel bag, takes off her coat. The blonde places everything on a table.

THE HOSTESS: Follow me.

Both women go into a small lift. Mellie has no idea where she is being taken. The tall Scandinavian does not look at her anymore, but, with a vacant stare, drums on the wooden panelling with very long fingernails.

The lift arrives at a floor.

The door in front of them slides open and Mellie finds herself on a landing hung with heavy tapestries. The atmosphere is stifling and sophisticated, like the hostess.

The tall blonde now scratches at a door with the tips of her nails. Without waiting for a reply, she enters. Curtains of red velvet part to reveal another woman, another blonde, her hair artfully arranged, wearing a very décolleté dress of the same red as the curtains. This woman is even taller than the hostess, and if anything more beautiful, with an arrogant and somewhat languid air, and grey or green eyes that take in all of Mellie at a glance.

MELLIE (*murmuring*): You are Tania Legauff?

A tiny nod of assent.

TANIA: It was you who telephoned me?

MELLIE: Yes.

The other woman steps aside to let Mellie into a room where everything is red and orange and aggressively luxurious.

The hostess leaves without a word, the curtains fall together, the door is shut.

TANIA: How did you find me?

MELLIE (*overcoming her embarrassment*): I went to the restaurant in the Eiffel Tower, then to a photographer. He gave me your phone number.

The tall blonde has seated herself at a small dressing table and is gluing false lashes onto her eyelids.

MELLIE: But I haven't much time. I have to catch another plane.

TANIA: You've gone to a lot of trouble to see me!

MELLIE (*solemnly*): They arrested your sister, last night.

No reply. No reaction whatsoever.

MELLIE: I know that she isn't guilty.

The other woman looks at her for a second in one of the mirrors that surround her. She shrugs her bare shoulders.

TANIA: So what?

At first Mellie says nothing. Then she raises her voice a little.

MELLIE: What do you mean, 'so what'? She's your sister!

TANIA (*rising calmly*): So what?

Mellie grabs her by the arms, impatiently. The other woman does not defend herself.

MELLIE: I want her to be set free! You hear me? Free!

Tania looks down at the hands gripping her bare arms. She looks up again at Mellie with strange, heavy eyes. She is not in the least upset.

TANIA (*softly*): Well, isn't my sister the lucky one …

Mellie lets go of her, repelled by the ambiguity of her gaze.

Tania rubs her arms.

TANIA (*in a more friendly, intimate voice*): I haven't the slightest idea what you're talking about. Sit down. Tell me who you are.

She pushes Mellie gently, but firmly, towards a kind of square platform-bed in the centre of the room.

Mellie sits down apprehensively on the edge of the bed, over which is spread a fur cover. Tania kneels beside her, in her false eyelashes, her red evening gown, her lacquered coiffure. Mellie does not look at her, and is obviously uncomfortable, on the defensive.

TANIA: Give me your hand.

Hesitantly, Mellie holds out her left hand. Tania looks at her wedding-ring, then her chewed fingernails. Mellie pulls her hand away.

Smiling indulgently, Tania draws quite close to Mellie to speak to her in a low and faintly scolding voice.

TANIA: You know what it means when a girl bites her nails?

Looking her in the eye, Mellie becomes even more nervous and turns away.

Tania laughs lightly, in amusement.

TANIA (*softly*): Don't make such a face, it's not a sin.

MELLIE (*defending herself*): I didn't come here to talk about sin!

Silence. They look at each other, one sitting, the other kneeling.

TANIA (*gently*): When people bite their nails, it's not what you think. It means they haven't grown up and are still ruled by their imaginations. (*Pause.*) What did you come to see me about?

MELLIE: Where was your sister, Tuesday evening?

TANIA: Mado? Here, as usual.

MELLIE (*confused*): Here? In Paris? … But why didn't you tell that to the police?

Tania looks at her intently, wondering if this little country mouse is simply pretending, after all, to be so foolish.

TANIA: You tell me. You think this is the sort of place that wants the police around?

Mellie does not reply.

TANIA: Answer me.

MELLIE: I'd have to know where I am, first!

Worn out by so much naïveté, the tall blonde stands up again.

MELLIE: Who was your sister with, Tuesday night?

TANIA (*in an artificial tone*): Some people.

MELLIE: I want to see them.

Tania looks at her for a few seconds without saying anything, torn between compassion and irritation.

TANIA: That's easy.

She opens a door at the other end of the room and leaves.

Mellie stands up, paces back and forth, waiting. She pulls the red curtain aside, lets it fall back into place. She is beginning to understand where she is: in a high-class bordello.

Perhaps she had already suspected as much, without daring to admit it to herself.

The door at the far end of the room opens again. Tania enters with three men. The one who comes in first, the one who is the most nonchalant, the most elegant in his black cashmere dinner jacket, is Monsieur. He is not called anything else. He has the handsome face of a man of about forty, sure of himself, who never loses his nerve.

The other two – a Marco with a beard, a Dominique with a long, alarming face – are thugs.

TANIA: Here she is.

MONSIEUR: Ah!

He walks over to Mellie, who has turned towards him. She has no idea what is going on.

TANIA: I feel as though I were playing with dolls.

Monsieur grabs a handful of Mellie's hair, forcing her head back. He has a deep, beautiful voice, and is quite relaxed. He is frightening.

125

MONSIEUR: These days, dollies can talk. What does this one say?

TANIA (*behind him*): She's asking questions.

MONSIEUR: Ah!

He still has Mellie by the hair. He studies her carefully. He smiles at her. He is even more frightening when he smiles.

28

Sweating, dishevelled, so drunk she no longer knows where she is, Mellie crawls on her hands and knees along a labyrinthine path traced in white chalk on a gleaming parquet floor.

She is in an empty ballroom in a semi-basement illuminated by lamps with ornate 1920s shades, very Jazz Age.

She is in hell.

MONSIEUR: Where were we?

He is leaning back against a mahogany bar, speaking to Marco, who sits straddling a chair.

MARCO (*intoning solemnly*): Her father had gone off with the mattress ticking. Then she took a plane with sixty thousand dollars in an envelope …

MONSIEUR (*to Mellie*): Where is that envelope?

A lighted cigarette suddenly appears in front of the young woman, who stops in her tracks.

At the other end of the long ivory cigarette holder is Dominique. Mellie looks up at Monsieur with sweat trickling down her face and desperation in her eyes.

MELLIE (*blurting out her words*): I posted it!

MONSIEUR: To whom?

She hesitates. Dominique slowly waves his cigarette holder in front of her.

MELLIE (*afraid*): To myself … In Le Cap-des-Pins!

The three men look at one another resignedly.

MONSIEUR (*carelessly*): Off with her head!

From his jacket pocket he pulls a small pillbox, which he opens, taking his time.

MONSIEUR (*patiently*): You flew to Paris to send yourself a letter back in Le Cap-des-Pins, is that it?

MELLIE: No … (*Explaining.*) Two Americans were following me at Orly! I had to get rid of the money!

MONSIEUR (*taking his pill*): Why were these two Americans following you?

MELLIE (*as though this was obvious*): Because of Harry Dobbs!

MONSIEUR: Harry Dobbs. Ah! … And may I know who this new character is?

MELLIE: An American colonel.

Resigned looks are again exchanged among the three men. Monsieur presses his fingertips to his eyelids with an air of exquisite weariness.

MONSIEUR: What I have the most trouble understanding is what your connection with Sacchi might be. Could you describe him for us?

Mellie, at her wits' end, is unable to get out a single word. The cigarette holder becomes menacing.

MELLIE: He was very tall!

MONSIEUR: Ah! … And that's all?

MELLIE (*giving up on explanations*): Hand me my coat, I'll show you.

Monsieur nods to Marco, who is the closest to the coat, which is now lying on a chair along with the travel bag. Marco brings the coat to the young woman, who feels around in one pocket, pulling out the two walnuts Dobbs had placed there.

Mellie gets painfully to her feet and staggers towards a window next to the mahogany bar.

Trying to seem brave, she tosses the walnuts up and down in her hand.

The three men watch her, intrigued.

When she is a few yards from the window, she stops, takes a

deep breath, and with as much strength as she can still muster, hurls a walnut against the panes. One of them shatters in a great cascading crash.

As her dumbfounded audience looks on, she then picks up a glass sitting half-full on the bar. She is teetering dangerously.

MELLIE: When you break the window, that means you're in love.

She takes a swig of alcohol and sets down the drink.

MELLIE (*proudly*): He's the one who always said that!

At the same moment, on the floor above, Harry Dobbs makes his entrance.

The same hostess greets him.

HOSTESS (*simply*): This way, please.

She goes up the steps of an imposing stone staircase, followed by Dobbs. He does not even glance around. He has understood where he is.

The red curtains part once more to reveal Tania standing in the doorway of her room, waiting for her client.

Dobbs pulls a note from the breast pocket of his jacket and holds it above his shoulder, without turning around. The hostess takes the money and immediately withdraws.

Motionless, Dobbs looks Tania straight in the face for a long time.

DOBBS: Where is she?

Tania merely blinks her false eyelashes, once. Silence.

Dobbs covers her face with his right hand and coldly pushes her backwards. Stunned, she loses her balance, but before she can regain it he does the same thing again with his left hand, more brutally, and sends her reeling onto the bed.

DOBBS (*his voice raised*): Where is she?

TANIA (*rallying*): I don't know what you're talking about!

Then Dobbs turns mean. He grabs the tall blonde woman by her ankles, pulls her off the bed, yanks her to her feet, and shoves her towards the door so that she can show him the way.

Below, on the dance floor, women are not having any easier a time of it. Mellie's eyes are closed from exhaustion, yet by some miracle she is still on her feet, a pathetic puppet whom Marco and Dominique are stubbornly and methodically passing between them, back and forth, watched by the inscrutable Monsieur.

Suddenly a double door flies open and Tania, pushed from behind, is sent stumbling noisily to the back of the room. After her comes Dobbs, looking grim, as steady and determined as a bulldozer.

When he appears, the two thugs let go of Mellie, who totters in one more little circle before crumpling to the floor in a half-faint.

Then everything happens very fast. Mellie blinks desperately at jarring images from a bad dream: Dominique rushing at Dobbs, who deals with him and then punches Marco with both fists. Then Marco, falling backwards, smashes through a decorative railing of black wood and snatches up one of its broken rods to use as a weapon; but Dobbs wrests it from him, Marco grabs another, and they face each other like gladiators, under the still imperturbable gaze of Monsieur, who has no intention of spoiling his cashmere jacket.

Nothing is real anymore.

DOBBS (*to Monsieur*): Tell him to drop it!

MONSIEUR (*to Marco*): That's enough.

His henchman obeys, tossing the wooden rod onto the floor. Dobbs is not playing fair, perhaps, but he takes this opportunity to swing his own bar at Marco's belly, dropping his opponent to the floor, bent neatly in two. When he is in a bad mood, and worried about a little bourgeois housewife whom he has got into very hot water, Dobbs dispenses with the niceties.

Monsieur has not so much as twitched. One might almost take him to be amused to see his bodyguards littering the parquet. After all, he is not paying them to shoot marbles. He placidly swallows a pill.

Her hair glued to her temples with perspiration, Mellie has opened her eyes to see Harry Dobbs bending over her. She sees he is concerned. She manages a faint smile.

MELLIE (*murmuring*): I'm really glad to see you, Mr Dobbs.

She holds out to him the walnut she still has in her hand.

DOBBS (*softly*): Same here, Love Love.

He lifts up the young woman and holds her standing against him, her cheek on his shoulder.

He helps her into her white coat.

Marco and Dominique have got to their feet and just glare at Dobbs in silence. Tania, in her red dress, has remained quietly off to one side with her hair only very slightly messed.

MONSIEUR (*serenely*): Since you truly do exist, Mr Dobbs, would you tell me at last what this game is all about? … It's been more than a year since Mr Sacchi and I parted company.

DOBBS (*sincerely*): It's a misunderstanding. And it's all my fault.

He turns to leave. Seeing that Mellie will not be able to walk, he carries her to the door in his arms. As they pass Tania, the tall blonde picks up the little travel bag, which has been sitting on a chair, and places it disdainfully in Mellie's lap.

29

A long corridor in a grand hotel in Paris: the Prince de Galles, or Le Meurice.

Preceded by a concierge holding the leather travel bag, Dobbs marches along, still carrying Mellie.

It is almost four in the morning.

The concierge opens a door and steps aside. Dobbs sets Mellie down on her feet in the middle of the room, holding her against him, because she is asleep standing up. He tips the concierge.

CONCIERGE: Will you be needing anything, sir?

DOBBS: No, thanks. (*Changing his mind.*) Yes, actually. Have some coffee sent up at eight o'clock.

CONCIERGE: Yes, sir. Thank you, sir.

When the door has closed behind him, Dobbs takes Mellie's face in his hands. Her eyelids flutter half-open. She cannot walk and clings to him.

DOBBS (*patiently*): You have to get home before your husband returns, Love Love. I'll take you back ... Are you listening?

He can see that she is not. If he were to let go of her, she would drop into a heap. He sighs.

A few moments later, having taken off his jacket, he manoeuvres the young woman, still in her wrinkled white dress, into the shower cubicle. He holds her upright, and turns on the tap.

At first she is scared when the water startles her awake. Then she sees Dobbs, understands what is happening, and welcomes the shower spray. Through the soaking strands of hair straggling across her face, she smiles at him, gratefully.

And the water keeps pouring down, cleansing her of everything.

Saturday, 8 a.m.

30

The first glimmers of daylight filter into the room.

Mellie is wearing one of the hotel's white towelling dressing gowns. Lying on a sofa, she is dozing before a low table on which sits a tray bearing a delicious breakfast. Her hair is still damp. Her face is smooth, almost childlike.

Across the room, Dobbs is speaking on the telephone, holding a cup in his other hand. His voice is low, but Mellie opens her eyes and listens to him.

DOBBS (*in English*): Give me until this evening, Günther ... I'm telling you, I'm going to win ... No, she's here ... Right, until this evening.

He hangs up, takes a swig of coffee. Turning his head, he notices that Mellie is awake. He comes over to sit next to her, with a quiet little smile. There is no sound outside the room, which is bathed in a milky blue light.

Dobbs pours a cup of coffee. Mellie takes it, drinking as she watches him spread butter on a piece of bread.

DOBBS: You should eat something.

She takes the piece of bread and butter. He makes himself another one.

MELLIE (*softly*): I heard what you were saying.

DOBBS (*same tone*): It's my job, Love Love.

She nods, and settles herself more comfortably on the sofa.

MELLIE: You live here?

DOBBS: In Germany. But all hotel rooms look alike.

Mellie eats her bread and butter; Dobbs eats his.

MELLIE: I saw a picture of a little boy in your suitcase. Is he yours?

DOBBS (*proudly*): Yes.

MELLIE: You're married?

He shakes his head.

DOBBS: Single father.

He smiles. So does she.

MELLIE (*suddenly solemn*): You're really sure you're going to win, Mr Dobbs?

At that moment, there is a knock on the door. Before going to open it, he makes a point of replying.

DOBBS: I should not have used that word.

He rises and goes over to the door, still holding the rest of his bread and butter.

MELLIE (*in a low voice*): I didn't kill him.

He looks back at her for a second. He sighs; nothing more. Reaching through the half-open door with his free hand, he takes something being held out to him.

DOBBS: Thanks.

It is Mellie's white dress, washed and pressed, on a hanger. He closes the door.

DOBBS: Are you able to get dressed?

Mellie nods. He drapes the dress delicately over the back of a chair, and, finishing his bread and butter, goes out into the hall, leaving her alone.

In her eyes, at this moment, is a tenderness that may well be called affection.

31

M arseille–Marignane.
  Like a great shining bird, a jet lands on a runway in the bright noonday sunshine.

Tony appears in his navy-blue uniform, suitcase in hand, coming down the stairs from the crew area in the terminal.

He is astonished when Mellie grabs him by the arm at the foot of the stairs.

TONY: You came to meet me?

She kisses him and hugs him tightly, with a great feeling of comfort. She is wearing the same clothes she had on in Paris, but she has combed her hair and applied fresh makeup.

MELLIE: I wanted to talk to you before you see the house.

Tony looks at her and can tell from her dejected face that something serious has happened while he has been gone.

MELLIE: I had a fight with Mummy … A terrible fight. She even broke a door.

TONY (*shocked*): A door! … But why?

MELLIE (*shamelessly*): Because of my father.

For Tony, this subject is clearly taboo. He nods in understanding.

He puts his arm around Mellie and leads her off towards the car park.

TONY: Don't worry about it. A door can be mended. And I'm leaving for London this evening.

MELLIE: Oh, no!

TONY: Oh, yes!

Standing behind the plate-glass partition at an airport ticket desk, Harry Dobbs watches without expression as they walk off, close together, towards the Dodge left in the car park the previous evening.

32

Afternoon sunshine in the garden at Tony and Mellie's house.

A postman on a bicycle hands Juliette the large brown envelope containing the sixty thousand dollars sent via express mail.

Juliette tips the postman. As he rides off, she notices Dobbs on the other side of the road, opposite the front gate. He is standing stock still, observing her silently.

Juliette turns away and walks quickly back to the house.

In the vast living room reigns the special atmosphere of a place where people have been playing cards for hours.

Tony, Toussaint, and two other friends are sitting around a table having their regular Saturday game. Another man is seated behind Toussaint, watching him play.

There are glasses, overflowing ashtrays, and the men have all taken off their jackets.

They are playing without a word, except for the occasional 'Pass' or 'Raise you ten'.

Tony looks up when Juliette crosses the front hall, but he returns immediately to his hand.

She goes upstairs with the brown envelope.

Mellie is sleeping on her bed with a blanket over her. Juliette draws back the curtains and sits down near her daughter. Fondly, she watches her sleep for a moment. She strokes her forehead.

JULIETTE (*very quietly, to herself*): Mélancolie Mau ... You're sending yourself letters, now?

Mellie opens her eyes with a little start.

MELLIE: Huh? What did you say?

JULIETTE: Nothing ... This came for you. That is your writing, isn't it?

Mellie does not reply. She takes the envelope, looking around her in some surprise.

MELLIE: What time is it?

JULIETTE: You slept all afternoon.

While her daughter gets up and puts on a dressing gown, Juliette goes over to the door and fiddles with the dangling lock.

JULIETTE: Is this the door I broke? ... Hmm, I'm stronger than I thought!

Mellie has turned towards her anxiously.

MELLIE: Did you tell Tony it wasn't true?

Juliette looks at her for a moment before answering, with that air of stern indifference she likes to put on.

JULIETTE (drily): What do you think?

Mellie lowers her eyes.

JULIETTE: And you're forgetting everything these days.

MELLIE: What have I done now?

JULIETTE: Toussaint asked you to speak to Tony about a loan.

MELLIE: Oh, tuba! It completely slipped my mind! Is he upset?

JULIETTE: Certainly not. He's in quite a good mood today.

She opens the door with the broken lock to return downstairs, but looks back once more.

JULIETTE: That woman they arrested has confessed everything!

The face Mellie turns towards her mother is distorted by pain, as though she had received an electric shock.

Fortunately, Juliette has already gone.

A moment later, in the kitchen, the young woman puts the bus passenger's red bag away in the cupboard over the sink. She crumples up the brown envelope, now empty, and tosses it into the dustbin.

She has put on her dress and her white boots.

140

She is going towards the back door when Toussaint comes suddenly into the kitchen carrying two large empty beer bottles.

TOUSSAINT: Afternoon, Mellie! … Hot, isn't it?

She manages to conceal her anxiety. He places the bottles on the table.

MELLIE: I'm so sorry, Toussaint, I forgot all about it.

TOUSSAINT: Oh, it doesn't matter. I'm doing very well at the moment.

He runs water from the sink tap over his face, as though he were entirely at home in her house.

Mellie gets him a towel from a cupboard.

TOUSSAINT: Thanks.

While he dries his face, she tries to think how she can bring up the subject that is troubling her.

MELLIE (*abruptly*): The woman didn't look guilty!

He stops rubbing his face and looks at her. He knows almost immediately which woman she means.

TOUSSAINT (*with a sigh*): Listen, Mellie. She killed her lover in some quarrel over a lot of money and buried him at La Pelouque. Period.

MELLIE (*astounded*): Buried? (*Pause.*) She buried him? … But when?

TOUSSAINT: Last year, imagine!

Mellie could not be more staggered if the ceiling had fallen on her head. Toussaint is rummaging through the bottles in the fridge and does not notice how disconcerted she is.

MELLIE: I spoke to that Colonel Dobbs … I must have misunderstood …

TOUSSAINT: That business has nothing to do with it! Dobbs is looking for a mental patient who escaped from an army hospital in Germany. Convicted three times for rape and this time he ran off with all the hospital's cash. Is there any more beer?

141

MELLIE (*ignoring his question*): And you're conducting an inquiry?

TOUSSAINT (*dismissively*): What inquiry? … Dobbs is convinced his nutcase got up to his old tricks around here and that he's dead. But we've had no complaint lodged and no body found. I even bet him a hundred francs that his man's still on the run … So there's no more beer?

MELLIE: I'll go and get some.

TOUSSAINT: Thanks, Mellie. (*On his way out of the kitchen.*) They're weird, these Americans. They're looking for a fresh corpse, they bring in dogs from Toulon, and they dig up an old one! Funny, huh?

Mellie has turned away. She nods in agreement, but he cannot see her face. Smiling, he goes off to join the others, leaving her there, more worried than ever.

33

Out in the garden, the sun is setting behind the trees. There are several cars parked in the drive, including Toussaint's blue sedan.

Coming out by the kitchen door, Mellie runs towards the Dodge in her white raincoat, holding the red bag with one arm and the empty beer bottles with the other. She gets into the station-wagon and puts everything down on the seat beside her.

On the narrow road to Le Cap-des-Pins, she notices Dobbs's red Mustang parked on the hard shoulder, two or three hundred yards from the house. She looks at the Mustang as she drives by, but the American is nowhere to be seen.

Ten minutes later, she stops on the small, rugged, grassy promontory where she disposed of the body.

She sits still for a moment, looking out through the windscreen. The sun is low on the horizon, over the sea. The wind has risen, bringing with it a stormy sky. There is no one in sight.

Mellie picks up the red bag and opens the car door to get out.

At that instant, in the shadowy interior of the car, an arm reaches out from behind her seat to grab her shoulder.

Mellie freezes, stifling a cry.

It is Dobbs. Thinking fast, Mellie heaves a great sigh of relief. After reaching out to close her car door again, Dobbs leans his elbows on the back of her seat. He flashes her his satisfied smile.

DOBBS: I was right, Love Love. You brought him home with you in the car, Tuesday evening. Except that you didn't know it.

MELLIE (*enraged*): I hate you! ... Liar! ... Cheater! ... You had nothing on me! … You set it all up, with your rotten tomcat smile!

DOBBS (*placidly*): You're the one who got mixed up. As soon as I saw you look at the newspaper, in the church, I knew I'd get you.

MELLIE: Never!

DOBBS (*shrugging*): You've led me to MacGuffin.

MELLIE: Who?

DOBBS: Your victim. His name was MacGuffin. (*Pointing to the sea.*) I'm sure he's out there. I'll have the bottom dragged.

Silence.

MELLIE (*more calmly*): I wanted some fresh air … Even if you find him here, that's no proof!

Dobbs shakes his head reproachfully.

DOBBS: Love Love!

He is sitting in the back seat, completely relaxed.

DOBBS: And the bag you're holding – that's not proof?

Mellie does not need to think twice. She immediately throws the bag as hard as she can out of her open window. It vanishes over the precipice.

MELLIE (*laughing nervously*): What bag? … I haven't any bag!

Dobbs replies with a deep sigh. He gets out of the car, slamming the door behind him. He walks towards the edge of the cliff.

Mellie does not waste a second. She starts up the Dodge and drives off, leaving him behind.

34

Coming out of the living room, Juliette puts on her coat, a cigarette dangling from her lips.

The sound of car engines can be heard outside.

Juliette enters the kitchen and finds Mellie there, in her unbuttoned raincoat, leaning back against the door to the garden. Juliette is startled by the hunted look on her daughter's face.

JULIETTE: They're going.

Mellie straightens up immediately and tries to hide her distress.

JULIETTE: I can stay here tonight, if you like.

Mellie shakes her head slowly. She starts to take off her raincoat with a preoccupied air but stops to look at her mother.

MELLIE: I'm tired, that's all.

And then, automatically, she puts her raincoat back on again without realizing what she is doing. Smoking her cigarette, Juliette watches her, more worried than she appears.

JULIETTE: (*softly*): Mellie!

She says her name in a gentle, chiding tone, the way one speaks to a little girl.

MELLIE (*alarmed*): Now what have I done?

JULIETTE: Nothing, darling.

She goes over to her daughter, kisses her on the cheek, and turns to the door to leave. All of a sudden, Mellie throws herself into her mother's arms. She does not cry, or sob, or speak. She simply hugs her mother tight.

JULIETTE (*taken aback*): Well, my goodness!

They stay motionless, like that, for long seconds.

A police siren out in the driveway shatters the silence.

Mellie lifts her head, an agony of fear in her eyes.

TONY (*entering the kitchen*): Bah! That's Toussaint leaving. His siren's stuck.

Mellie lets go of her mother and turns away, trying to compose herself.

TONY (*to Juliette*): I'm off to London this evening. Why don't you stay with her?

JULIETTE: Certainly not, since you're taking her with you.

TONY (*amazed*): I am? What's the occasion?

Looking at her mother, Mellie is also surprised, but already regaining her confidence; because running away is in fact one solution to her problem.

JULIETTE: I know Mélancolie ... She'll find you a good reason before I drive through the gate ... (*Touching Mellie's cheek.*) She's unbeatable.

Juliette opens the door to the garden and steps outside, tossing away her cigarette.

JULIETTE (*before closing the door behind her*): At the gate, I'll beep my horn!

Tony follows his wife as she walks towards the stairs. He stops at the bottom of the steps, looking annoyed.

TONY: Listen, sweetie, this is silly.

She leans down towards him, holding onto the bannister.

MELLIE (*very softly*): Silly or not, you're taking me along ... I want to stay with you ... I have things to tell you ... Far away from here!

There is such supplication in her voice that he lowers his head, finally resigned.

TONY: All right, sweetie.

Juliette's horn can be heard as she drives through the gate, going 'Beep-beep!'

35

It will soon be twilight, under heavy clouds.

On top of the promontory, there are searchlights, parked cars, policemen coming and going, an utter circus.

Below, on the shore pounded by waves, lies the body of the passenger from the bus. He is stretched out face down on a flat rock in his soaking and unbuttoned raincoat.

Dobbs is bending over the corpse. A police frogman is speaking to Dobbs while he peels off his wetsuit.

FROGMAN: He was wedged beneath the rocks. It would have been months before he surfaced.

Toussaint joins them, with another plainclothes policeman. He pulls a hundred francs from his wallet.

TOUSSAINT: You've won your bet, Colonel.

Dobbs takes the money, puts it in the breast pocket of his jacket. He speaks to the frogman, who is walking away.

DOBBS: Tell them to give me some light, from up there.

Toussaint crouches by the body, looking gloomy.

TOUSSAINT: If he started in on some woman around here and got himself killed, you've had it, Colonel.

DOBBS: Why?

TOUSSAINT: Because. (*Pause.*) He won't be talking anymore. So good luck finding out what happened!

DOBBS (*ironically*): Just read my report.

Toussaint nods, looks at the other policeman, and stands up. Then the two of them go off along the path leading to the top of the cliff.

A powerful searchlight now beams down on the spot where Dobbs is standing next to the body, making the area as bright as day.

Dobbs blinks in the glare.

And then he bends down once again over the dead man. Wounds in the back. Arms stretched out above his head. The right hand is closed, tightly clenched. Dobbs struggles to open it, one finger after another.

He succeeds.

The passenger from the bus still holds in his hand the crystal button torn from Mellie's dress.

Dobbs takes it, studies it for an instant, and now he is the one who grips it in his fist. This time, he has found what he was looking for, and no mistake.

36

Tony, in uniform, places two suitcases in the back of the station-wagon and walks over to the gate, which the wind has blown half shut.

As he goes by, he caresses Mellie's cheek. She is sitting in the driver's seat in a light-coloured coat – a coat from before all this happened.

Suddenly she hears a police siren in the distance, approaching rapidly. She looks up, panic in her eyes.

Its rooflight whirling, Toussaint's car stops at the entrance to the driveway, barring the gate.

The siren stops when the engine is turned off.

Mellie has flung herself back against her seat. She waits, knowing she is lost.

Through the windscreen, she sees Dobbs appear, alone, at a bend in the drive. He comes towards her, walking at a leisurely pace, carrying the red bag in one hand.

Her heart racing, she watches him come closer, right up to her car door. He is smiling his cat smile. For a moment, they look silently into each other's eyes. He puts the bag on the roof of the car and leans down.

MELLIE (*carefully*): Have you finished your work?

DOBBS: I have the money, I have the body … Enough to write my report.

Her heart in her mouth, she waits for the rest. He is looking at her kindly, but she knows he is leading up to a crushing blow.

On the contrary, he sighs.

DOBBS: You can't have everything, right?

Mellie is not sure she understands.

DOBBS: And anyway, no one really wants to stir up this whole business.

Still looking at her, he takes something from his jacket pocket. He shows her, held between his thumb and forefinger, the tiny crystal button. A kind of moan catches in her throat.

Silence. Delicately, Dobbs takes her hand, places the button on her palm, closes her fingers around it.

DOBBS: The truth died with MacGuffin.

She lifts her eyes to his, without moving, without saying a word, but the nightmare is over. Her face shines with gratitude, with a joy she still hardly dares believe in, and with the sparkle of tears.

He strokes the young woman's fingers for a moment.

DOBBS (*gently*): Let your nails grow, Love Love.

He moves away, collecting the red bag from the roof of the car, never taking his eyes off Mellie.

DOBBS: Goodbye.

MELLIE (*hurriedly*): Mr Dobbs! … (*Smiling.*) A little while ago my mother called me Mélancolie!

DOBBS: Wonderful!

Tony has just appeared at the bend in the drive. Sensing his approach, the American pulls himself from the young woman's gaze.

He walks off with his usual confident, even step. Mellie watches him go, then looks down at the crystal button in her open hand. She is laughing and yet her eyes remain filled with tears. Torn like that between joy and heartache, she bows her head until it rests against the steering wheel.

37

A few moments later, Harry Dobbs is walking at the edge of the road that runs beside the sea. Carrying his bag, he is going off alone, in the twilight, to the Ford Mustang he left parked a little further on.

He hears the Dodge come up behind him but does not turn around.

When the station-wagon goes by, it is Tony who is driving. Sitting next to her husband, Mellie turns, and so does Dobbs. Their eyes meet, in a long look, one last time.

And then the Dodge speeds away.

Dobbs watches it drive away, disappear. He pulls a walnut from his jacket pocket, and stops in his tracks. He tells himself it is probably the one Mellie gave back to him, in a sordid place in Paris. He tosses it up and down in his hand, looking around him.

He has just walked by a shabby concrete house standing empty until the spring, with big windows smeared with white paint. He turns and walks back to it.

He intends to throw the walnut, but at the last moment he hesitates, changes his mind. He no longer wants to, or else it brings back memories he would rather forget.

Setting out again, he flings the nut – and the memories – over his shoulder, with a determined, decisive toss.

Behind him, a window smashes to bits.

Dobbs whips around, thunderstruck.

Staring at the damage, he cannot believe his eyes. And then he nods resignedly, and looks back down the road, where Mellie vanished.

DOBBS (*murmuring*): Bravo.

He starts walking back towards his car, carrying his red bag, alone, and doubtless a little sad.

Then, the storm that has been threatening for hours finally breaks, and rain begins to fall.

One Deadly Summer
Sébastien Japrisot

From a master of suspense comes this classic tale of lust
and revenge set in the French countryside.

Car mechanic Fiorimond is irresistibly drawn to the
beautiful, provocative Elle, a recent arrival in his sleepy
Provence village. Their relationship develops quickly, but
even as they make plans to marry, Fiorimond doesn't know
what to make of his bride-to-be: is she an enigma or simply
vacuous?

In fact, the troubled Elle is on a mission to exact revenge
on Fiorimond's family for a crime committed decades
earlier, with a plan that will ultimately destroy all their lives,
including hers...

ISBN: 9781910477502
e-ISBN: 9781910477519

The Lady in the Car with Glasses and a Gun
Sébastien Japrisot

A cult French crime classic of the 1960s, available in English
for the first time in 20 years.

Dany Longo is blonde, beautiful – and thoroughly un-
predictable. After doing a favour for her boss, she finds
herself behind the wheel of his exquisite Thunderbird on a
sun-kissed Parisian morning. On impulse she decides to head
south.

What started as an impromptu joyride rapidly takes a turn
for the chilling when strangers all along the unfamiliar route
swear they recognise Dany from the previous day. But that's
impossible: she was at work, she was in Paris, she was miles
away... wasn't she?

ISBN: 9781910477724
eISBN: 9781910477731

The Sleeping Car Murders
Sébastien Japrisot

A beautiful young woman lies sprawled on her berth in the sleeping car of the night train from Marseille to Paris. She is not in the embrace of sleep, or even in the arms of one of her many lovers. She is dead. And the unpleasant task of finding her killer is handed to overworked, crime-weary police detective Pierre 'Grazzi' Grazziano, who would rather play hide-and-seek with his little son than cat and mouse with a diabolically cunning, savage murderer.

ISBN: 9781910477939

e-ISBN: 9781910477991

Trap for Cinderella
Sébastien Japrisot

A young woman wakes up in a hospital room; what happened to her, and why, a mystery.

She remembers names: Michèle, Micky, or Mi, or perhaps Dominique or Do. Then the fire that destroyed her face, then the fall that punctured her head through which her memory leaks. And as she struggles to rebuild her identity, so too does she start to recall the crime that was commited.

But who has woken in that hospital room: the murderer or the victim?

ISBN: 9781913547127
e-ISBN: 9781913547141